In One Bed...
and Out the Other

by Mawby Green
and Ed Feilbert

Based on the French farce
Une Nuit Chez Vous... Madame!
by Jean de Letraz

A SAMUEL FRENCH ACTING EDITION

SAMUEL
FRENCH
FOUNDED 1830

New York Hollywood London Toronto

SAMUELFRENCH.COM

CHARACTERS

Maurice

Huguette Dubois

Gaston Dubois

Didier

Clara

Rosine

Aunt Alice

3

The action takes place in Paris in the drawing room of Monsieur and Madame Dubois. The time is the present.

ACT ONE

An autumn afternoon

ACT TWO

Only a few minutes later

ACT THREE

After dinner

In One Bed . . .
and Out the Other

ACT ONE

SCENE: *The drawing room of* MONSIEUR *and* MADAME
DUBOIS' *large and rambling garden apartment in
Paris.*

*A door downstage right leads to the study. Further
upstage along the right wall is a fireplace. The
right wall angles upstage and left forming a large
archway, with a platform below reached by a
single step. Upstage through the archway are
double doors, which lead to other parts of the
apartment: the main entrance, kitchen, etc. In
front of the double doors is a hall leading off
stage right to the dining room. Against the wall
left of the archway are a straightback chair and
a cabinet. The wall then recesses into French
windows, giving on to a terrace. The French
windows are essentially stage center. Left of the
French windows is a long platform reached on
either side by circular stairs of three steps each.
The right circular stairs come down at approx-
imately left center; the left circular stairs come
down at far left and face on stage. Upstage center*

on the platform is the door to MADAME DUBOIS'
*boudoir. Angled at the left end of the platform
is the door to the* DUBOIS' *bedroom.*

*The furnishings are warm and inviting. Below the
platform is a long sofa with a coffee table in
front. Behind the sofa is a pedestal holding a vase
of red roses. Downstage center is a low octagonal
table. Two comfortable chairs occupy the space
at right center. In front of these chairs is a hassock. A telephone, bell and a vase with a single
red rose are on the cabinet. In the archway, at
the left, is a small stand with a very tall rubber
plant. Wall brackets are right and left and a
chandelier hangs in the center of the room.*

TIME: *An autumn afternoon.*

As the curtain rises, MAURICE, *wearing the white
gloves and long apron of a servant, enters from
the hall awkwardly carrying a tray with coffee
service for two. He is in a bad humor. He puts
down the tray on the coffee table, then pulls off
his gloves and throws them on a chair.*

MAURICE. What a job! What a life! What am I
doing here? (*He goes to the telephone but before
dialing looks to see that no one is coming.*) Hello?
. . . Yes, everything's fine. Just fine! But I warn
you I'm not putting up with this another day! Jump
in your car and wait at the cafe across the street
until I signal . . . I'll wave my handkerchief . . .
They're about to have coffee and take a siesta . . .
Do they go straight to sleep? What else does one do

when one takes a siesta? . . . You would but they're married. Goodbye! I hear them coming! (*He replaces the receiver.*) Me, a servant! It's incredible! (*He shouts down the hall.*) The coffee's ready! (GASTON *and* HUGUETTE DUBOIS *enter. She is chic and beautiful but very bourgeois. He is neither chic nor beautiful, just bourgeois. They are bored from the monotony of wedded bliss.*)

HUGUETTE. (*To* MAURICE.) Must you shout, Didier? Really, we are not what you would call exacting employers, but we do feel a servant should serve with servility. (*She sits on the far left of the sofa.*)

MAURICE. My view precisely!

GASTON. How lucky for us! Are these your gloves?

MAURICE. Yes.

GASTON. What are they doing on that chair?

MAURICE. Nothing.

GASTON. Pick them up!

MAURICE. With pleasure! (*He picks up his gloves, puts them under his arm, then picks up the tongs to put the sugar into the cups.*)

GASTON. And put them on! Put them on even when you're using the tongs to put the sugar into the cups. (*He sits on the far right of the sofa.*)

MAURICE. (*Aside.*) I'd like to put them . . . (*He drops the sugar tongs and as he picks them up, drops his gloves. As he straightens up, he bumps into the tray.*)

GASTON. Oh, leave it alone! You give me the shakes! Get out of here! (*As* MAURICE *starts to leave.*) Didier!

MAURICE. M'sieur?

GASTON. I stopped you in order to have the pleasure of telling you again to get out of here!

MAURICE. Very well! (*He waits.*) May I go?

GASTON. (*Raising his voice.*) I ordered you to go!

MAURICE. (*Sweetly sarcastic.*) That's what I thought you said the first time! (*He goes out down the hall.*)

GASTON. He's impossible!

HUGUETTE. (*Serving the coffee.*) Then why did you engage him? Why did you dismiss Joseph while I was away on holiday?

GASTON. (*A bit constrained.*) He'd taken to drink.

HUGUETTE. To drink? Joseph, who drank nothing but water?

GASTON. You've heard of galloping consumption? He got spontaneous alcoholism. Shall we change the subject?

HUGUETTE. If you wish, dear.

GASTON. We used to have the cat to talk about but since he scooted over the fence, we've nothing to discuss but the servant problem.

HUGUETTE. (*After a brief silence.*) Well, go on.

GASTON. No, it's your turn. You go on. (*Another silence.*)

HUGUETTE. (*An amiable reproach.*) So you have nothing you want to say to me?

GASTON. Business is good.

HUGUETTE. Oh.

GASTON. Wood is selling well. Logs particularly . . . round ones for fires. Nothing can take the place of a log . . . and they never go out of style. Yesterday's log looks like today's and today's log looks like tomorrow's because wood is wood and wood is eternal. Yes, it's a miracle the way trees grow log-shaped. There's nothing anybody can do about it.

HUGUETTE. Nothing.

GASTON. Trees grow log-shaped. (*Another silence.*)

HUGUETTE. Say something charming.

GASTON. What?

HUGUETTE. Tell me you love me.

GASTON. (*Mechanically, as he sips his coffee.*) I adore you. What about you?

HUGUETTE. Oh, yes.

GASTON. (*With no enthusiasm.*) It's wonderful we're so happy.

HUGUETTE. Deliriously happy.

GASTON. We longed for the perfect home . . . and we have it.

HUGUETTE. (*With a pout.*) Well, to be honest, I'm not mad keen about this furniture.

GASTON. You're not mad keen? I am surprised. After all, this furniture belonged to my father and mother.

HUGUETTE. I know, Gaston, but I do think I'd be happier with something different.

GASTON. What, for instance?

HUGUETTE. I don't know. Have you any ideas?

GASTON. None. (*They fall silent and gaze vacantly into space.* GASTON *whistles between his teeth.*)

HUGUETTE. Shall we take our siesta?

GASTON. Yes, I could use forty winks. (*They rise and go up the stairs towards their bedroom.* MAURICE *comes in from the hall.*) You may clear away, we've finished.

MAURICE. (*Peevishly.*) Oh, well, if you insist!

GASTON. What do you mean 'if I insist'? Huguette, I think I had better have a word with Didier.

HUGUETTE. Very well, Gaston. (*She goes into the bedroom.*)

GASTON. (*Coming down the right stairs.*) Now listen to me. I'm a patient man . . .

MAURICE. Yes, m'sieur . . .

GASTON. . . . but you're making me lose my temper! Do you realize that?

MAURICE. (*Very chummy.*) I certainly do and I feel that in your place . . .

GASTON. Never mind my place. Think of hanging on to your own. Have I made myself clear?

MAURICE. Perfectly.

GASTON. Good. (*He goes up the stairs.* MAURICE *carries the tray to the cabinet.*)

MAURICE. Oh, that reminds me, I forgot to tell you, Gaston . . .

GASTON. (*Correcting him.*) I forgot to tell *monsieur!*

MAURICE. You did? What? What did you forget to tell me, old boy?

GASTON. Old boy! Old boy! (*Charging down the stairs.*) You are discharged! Leave the house!

MAURICE. (*Blithely ignoring him.*) I forgot to tell monsieur that I found a gold cigarette case under this cushion.

GASTON. What cigarette case?

MAURICE. This one. (*He takes it from his pocket.*) It has a lovely name engraved on it . . . Clara.

GASTON. (*Alarmed.*) What did you say? Clara?

MAURICE. Yes, Clara.

GASTON. Give me that case!

MAURICE. M'sieur. (*He gives him the case.*)

GASTON. My God! What a thing to have lying around! (*He quickly pockets it.*)

MAURICE. Clara . . . hmm . . . not much like madame's name, is it?

GASTON. Didier, I discharged Joseph because he showed no discretion. He couldn't keep his mouth shut.

MAURICE. Really, monsieur, there's no reason for you to give me explanations.

GASTON. (*Giving him a fifty franc note.*) How about this? (MAURICE *looks at the denomination. It's not too bad, so he slips it into his pocket.*) The neighbors may try to imply I entertained a young lady here, while my wife was away on holiday. If they do, simply shrug your shoulders.

MAURICE. (*Shrugging shoulders.*) Like this, monsieur?

GASTON. Higher! (MAURICE *shrugs higher.*) That's it.

MAURICE. And if these same neighbors try to imply that this young lady was named Clara, how shall I frame my reply?

GASTON. Shrug higher!

MAURICE. A most suitable answer, monsieur! (*He shrugs still higher.*)

GASTON. And in appreciation of your understanding, I am personally going to give you a monthly bonus.

MAURICE. How much?

GASTON. How much?! How much?! I'm giving you a monthly bonus out of the goodness of my heart and you want to know . . .

MAURICE. (*Flatly.*) How much. A manservant likes to find himself a Clara once in awhile too, you know.

GASTON. (*Furiously.*) Oh you . . . you . . . !! (HUGUETTE *enters from the bedroom.*)

HUGUETTE. What's keeping you, Gaston?

GASTON. Nothing, my dear.

HUGUETTE. Have you finished your talk with Didier?

GASTON. Yes, I straightened him out. I'm hoping he'll stay with us a long time.

MAURICE. That depends.

HUGUETTE. On what? (*She comes down the stairs.*)

MAURICE. One or two conditions.

HUGUETTE. Which are?

MAURICE. I'd like my own bathroom for one thing.

HUGUETTE. Really?

MAURICE. Yes, madame. I've been feeling I must have one for the last three minutes.

HUGUETTE. Anything else?

MAURICE. A radio, stereo, color TV . . .

GASTON. (*To the audience.*) You are listening to a program called 'The Big Squeeze.'

MAURICE. Well, m'sieur?

GASTON. You shall have them.

HUGUETTE. Oh, Gaston, I must say . . . !

GASTON. No, you mustn't say I'm too generous. It's my nature to be kind. Now let us siesta, my sweet. (HUGUETTE *goes back into the bedroom.*)

MAURICE. And about time too! (GASTON *glowers at* MAURICE *before following* HUGUETTE *out.*) Now for the other one! (*He goes to the French windows and waves his handkerchief.*) Look! I'm waving my handkerchief! . . . (*He starts for the double doors.*) Imagine what my friends would say if they saw me in this get-up! Me . . . Maurice . . . the Vicomte de Corneblanche! (DIDIER *comes in through the French windows as* MAURICE *steps into the archway.* DIDIER *is handsome and debonair.*)

DIDIER. Good afternoon, my man!

MAURICE. (*Turning around.*) What are you doing coming in through there? I was going to open the door.

DIDIER. Ah, but that's the advantage of a garden apartment. The husband goes out through the front door as the lover comes in through the window.

MAURICE. What are you talking about? There's no lover. And the husband is in there! (*He points to the bedroom.* DIDIER *hangs his hat on* MAURICE's *hand as if it were a peg.*)

DIDIER. Yes, the bedroom. And that's the boudoir next to it. That's the study, of course. Yes, thanks to you, I feel I've lived in this apartment for years, though I've never set foot in the place before.

MAURICE. I'm glad you're satisfied. Now what about the second installment? The other five hundred francs. That was our agreement.

DIDIER. You shall have it.

MAURICE. Oh, if only I hadn't lost so much at the Races.

DIDIER. (*Ironically.*) It's a good thing you did. Otherwise, how could I help you?

MAURICE. By forcing me to take this job as a servant! Tell me, why do I have to pay for your paltry thousand francs with this hideous humiliation?

DIDIER. Oh, just an idea I had.

MAURICE. (*To the audience.*) Another crackpot idea from a novelist who turns his life into a novelette.

DIDIER. (*As though imparting a great secret.*) The reason I asked you to come here is because I'm in love with the mistress of this house.

MAURICE. You can't be serious! In love with Huguette Dubois?

DIDIER. Madly.

MAURICE. A woman you haven't spoken to?

DIDIER. That's right.

MAURICE. A woman you haven't seen?

DIDIER. That's wrong. I have seen Huguette Dubois. I follow her from a distance, worshipping the ground she walks on.

MAURICE. (*To the audience.*) I told you. Crackpot.

DIDIER. Well, to be absolutely truthful, I don't

know yet whether I love her but I do know I want her. And what's more, I shall get her!

MAURICE. You're barking up the wrong tree. Huguette Dubois is fidelity personified. You'll never get her to come to your apartment alone.

DIDIER. I know that. That's why I decided to move in here.

MAURICE. You're crazy! Move in here? I bet you never pull that one off.

DIDIER. A thousand francs, double or nothing.

MAURICE. It's a bet!

DIDIER. Oh, Maurice, thanks to you I know everything there is to know about Huguette. Her likes and dislikes, her temperament, her passion for red roses . . . that she's virtuous and bored. How can I lose?

MAURICE. Why didn't you tell me I was plotting against myself? (DIDIER *laughs.*) Go ahead, laugh! (*He imitates* DIDIER'S *laugh.*) But you don't think I used my own name when I applied for this post, do you? Not me . . . Maurice, the Vicomte de Corneblanche.

DIDIER. I should hope not.

MAURICE. But you need an identity card . . .

DIDIER. Of course.

MAURICE. So I used yours . . . borrowed from your pocket.

DIDIER. What!

MAURICE. (*Delighted.*) Surprised? I took this job in your name . . . Didier . . . Didier Larue. How do you like that?

DIDIER. Well, all that means, Maurice, is that over the years you have managed to borrow everything I own, including my name.

MAURICE. They heard us. They're coming. (GASTON *comes in from the bedroom, followed by* HUGUETTE.)

GASTON. Monsieur?

DIDIER. Monsieur . . . (*He bows.*) Madame. Your man informed me you were resting, so I'm doubly sorry for disturbing you without an appointment.

GASTON. May I ask your name?

DIDIER. Why, I am Maurice, the Vicomte de Corne-blanche . . . (MAURICE *chokes back his indignation.*) and I am honored to pay my respects.

GASTON. May I ask the reason for your unexpected call?

DIDIER. Yes, indeed. But it's rather personal . . .

GASTON. (*To* MAURICE.) Didier, you may go.

MAURICE. (*Deeply mortified.*) Very well, monsieur . . . (*As he passes* DIDIER.) since the Vicomte feels my presence is superfluous. (*He goes out down the hall.*)

DIDIER. I'm sure you understand I wouldn't come here like this without a good reason.

GASTON. Of course. It's going to be a cold winter and you want to make certain you're kept warm.

DIDIER. (*Looking at* HUGUETTE.) Well, that's one way of looking at it.

GASTON. You want to buy logs for your fire.

DIDIER. Well, no, monsieur. I'm here on a purely sentimental matter.

GASTON. How can it possibly concern us?

DIDIER. Fate, monsieur. Fate has decreed that you and your wife should be involved in this drama of my life. When I awoke this morning, I realized I had only one choice: come to see you . . . or die!

GASTON. Won't you sit down?

DIDIER. Thank you! You see, I once lived in this apartment.

HUGUETTE. Really? How delightful!

DIDIER. No, madame. How tragic. For here, under

this roof, I spent my most golden hours . . . with a woman I adored. But then we drifted apart and I realized . . . too late, as always . . . that life meant nothing without her.

HUGUETTE. And the lady?

DIDIER. She feels the same. I'm sure of it.

GASTON. Then why were you thinking of dying this morning?

DIDIER. Because last night I spoke to her. She said that if we were back in the magic of our old surroundings, the love that flickers might flare up again. But she feels it will only happen here . . . in this paradise of love.

HUGUETTE. It's like a novelette.

DIDIER. A very short novelette. I know what she suggests is impossible so there is nothing left for me to do but fade out of her life forever.

HUGUETTE. (*To* GASTON.) The poor boy!

DIDIER. When I leave here, I shall drive my car straight into a tree!

GASTON. Find an oak. It's harder than chestnut.

HUGUETTE. What exactly can we do for you?

DIDIER. If I could . . . no, the idea's ridiculous.

HUGUETTE. Tell me.

DIDIER. If only I could come back here for one night, madame.

HUGUETTE. For one night?

DIDIER. At a time.

GASTON. Monsieur, that's all very well but we're not prepared to move out just to please you.

DIDIER. Of course not! And you mustn't dream of it. It's unthinkable. (*He takes out an envelope from his pocket.*) Since I have no family, will you hand this envelope over to my lawyer?

GASTON. What's in it?

DIDIER. My will. May I entrust it to you, madame?

HUGUETTE. Oh no! I couldn't! It's too frightful!
. . . Gaston, I've had an inspiration! We don't have
to lend him the whole apartment. We can lend him
this room. Then he can invite this lady without disturbing us.

DIDIER. What a gracious, lovely idea! I was hoping
against hope it might occur to you.

HUGUETTE. It did! Oh, it did!

DIDIER. Ah, madame, we are so alike: you too feel
with the heart.

HUGUETTE. I do! Oh, I do!

GASTON. Have you ever tried selling insurance,
monsieur?

DIDIER. (*Choosing to misunderstand.*) Then you
agree? How wonderful!

HUGUETTE. Oh, Gaston, I can't tell you how happy
you've made me. (*She kisses him on the brow.*)

GASTON. (*Begrudgingly.*) Well, if it's a matter of
saving his life . . .

DIDIER. And I'm sure you won't mind if I make a
few changes.

GASTON. Such as?

DIDIER. Nothing really. Bring in some new furniture.

GASTON. New furniture?

HUGUETTE. Of course, new furniture! Why not?
(MAURICE *enters from the hall and hands* GASTON *a
business card.*)

MAURCE. A gentleman, m'sieur. I showed him into
the study.

GASTON. (*After looking at the card.*) Will you excuse
me?

DIDIER. By all means! Make yourself at home!
(GASTON *does a "double-take."*)

GASTON. (*To* HUGUETTE.) It's one of my biggest
accounts! (*From the Christmas carol, "Good King
Wenceslas," he sings:*) 'He's gathering winter fu-u-el!'
(*He goes into the study happily.*)

HUGUETTE. (*To* MAURICE.) Didier, Monsieur de
Corneblanche will be staying with us. See that he's
made comfortable.

MAURICE. (*Flabbergasted.*) What? Monsieur de
Corneblanche is moving in here?

DIDIER. That is correct, Didier. But I won't be
needing your services for the moment. You may go.

MAURICE. (*Controlling himself with difficulty.*) Very
well, monsieur. (*To the audience.*) There goes my one
thousand francs.

DIDIER. (*Aside, to* MAURICE.) Doubled!

MAURICE. (*Dolefully.*) Oh! (*He goes out down the
hall.*)

HUGUETTE. How do you propose changing this
room?

DIDIER. Why, to suit her.

HUGUETTE. How thoughtful of you!

DIDIER. Yes, everything I do will be to satisfy her.
Will you help me?

HUGUETTE. How do you mean?

DIDIER. Tell me, do you like it frilly or clean cut?

HUGUETTE. What?

DIDIER. Your bedroom.

HUGUETTE. Oh, I prefer it frilly.

DIDIER. So does she. What's your favorite color?

HUGUETTE. Cyclamen. I adore cyclamen.

DIDIER. You don't say! Her favorite, too.

HUGUETTE. So you intend turning this room into a
bedroom?

DIDIER. We turned every room into a bedroom, madame!

HUGUETTE. How exciting!

DIDIER. Then you'll help me?

HUGUETTE. Oh, yes! It will be so stimulating after the humdrum way we drag along here. (MAURICE *comes in with a vase of red roses. To* MAURICE.) What is it, Didier?

MAURICE. Flowers for madame.

HUGUETTE. Is there a card?

MAURICE. No, madame.

HUGUETTE. Whoever could have sent them?

DIDIER. I took the liberty. I mean, as a gesture of appreciation in case madame had been so kind as to hand the will over to my lawyer.

HUGUETTE. How lovely they are! Red roses!

MAURICE. They'd have looked nice on your coffin, monsieur. (*He goes out through the double doors.*)

DIDIER. My beloved's favorite flowers.

HUGUETTE. Mine, too!

DIDIER. (*In mock surprise.*) This time I refuse to believe it! You don't say! (MAURICE *re-enters.*)

MAURICE. I should like to say a visitor has arrived. A lady.

DIDIER. Then I must go and see about the furniture. Madame, I don't know how to thank you.

HUGUETTE. Make her happy. That's all I ask.

DIDIER. Make who happy?

HUGUETTE. Why . . . the lady you're going to love here, of course.

DIDIER. You can rely on me for *that*, madame. I shall do everything I can . . . leave no bed unturned. I mean 'au revoir,' madame . . . (*He goes out swiftly through the French windows.* HUGUETTE *goes up to the windows and stands there lost in a dream.*)

MAURICE. Madame has not forgotten the visitor?

HUGUETTE. What's that? Oh, yes, of course. Did she give her name?

MAURICE. Yes. She is Clara . . . Madame Clara Gauthier.

HUGUETTE. I don't know her.

MAURICE. (*Downstage, "shrugging higher" to the audience.*) No, I know you don't.

HUGUETTE. Oh, good heavens! She may be the lady Monsieur de Corneblanche is expecting. And now he's gone! Ask her to come in.

MAURICE. Yes, madame. (*He leaves through the double doors.*)

HUGUETTE. How lovely they are! Red roses! He's perfectly right. Done over, this could be a most charming room. (MAURICE *re-enters.*)

MAURICE. Madame Clara Gauthier! (CLARA, *a dazzling girl, rushes in.*)

CLARA. Here I am! I couldn't wait . . . (*She stops short, embarrassed at seeing* HUGUETTE.) Oh, madame . . .

HUGUETTE. Come in.

CLARA. Thank you. Oh, dear. I'm afraid I didn't expect . . .

HUGUETTE. To see me here?

CLARA. No, I don't think I did. I hardly know what to say . . .

HUGUETTE. Then don't say anything. I can guess who you are.

CLARA. You can?

HUGUETTE. Yes, I'm sure of it.

CLARA. Oh.

MAURICE. (*Who has been eavesdropping.*) Clara!

What a lovely summer pastime! (*He leaves through the double doors.*)

HUGUETTE. It's not the first time you've been in this room, is it?

CLARA. No . . . I can't say it is.

HUGUETTE. It must be full of memories for you.

CLARA. Very full.

HUGUETTE. I know how your emotions must be fluttering . . .

CLARA. Like a frightened bird.

HUGUETTE. Then let me put you at ease. I am the soul of discretion so don't let my presence embarrass or inhibit you in any way whatever. You must make yourself completely at home.

CLARA. How kind, how very kind!

HUGUETTE. Your lover is waiting for you impatiently!

CLARA. Oh, such ecstacy! No one has ever given me more wonderful news!

HUGUETTE. Here, in this room, you'll be able to . . . Yes. I place it entirely at your service.

CLARA. I don't know how to put my thanks into words.

HUGUETTE. Don't try. What a pleasure it will be to help do over this room for you! What joy to make you both happy! I want you to believe that.

CLARA. I do. Oh, I do! (GASTON *sweeps in from the study.*)

GASTON. (*Enthusiastically.*) Well, I've done it again! Another big ord . . . (*He catches sight of* CLARA *and flaps around the room.*) Oh! . . . Oh! . . . Oh! . . . Oh!

CLARA. (*Seeing him.*) Ah!

GASTON. Huguette?

HUGUETTE. Yes?

GASTON. Didier told me . . . told me you had a visitor . . . and so I . . .

HUGUETTE. How thoughtful to come in so quickly.

GASTON. Yes. I . . . I wonder if I might have a word in private with madame. (*He indicates* CLARA.)

HUGUETTE. Of course. And I don't have to tell you, I shall be delighted with anything you plan for her pleasure.

GASTON. (*Amazed.*) You will?

HUGUETTE. Yes. Anything at all! (*She goes into the boudoir, after a beaming smile for* CLARA.)

CLARA. Gaston!

GASTON. Clara!

CLARA. Are you pleased to see me again?

GASTON. I'm beside myself. But you should have warned me you were coming.

CLARA. Did I pick an awkward time?

GASTON. . . . No. Not at all. But I'd like to have been here when you arrived.

CLARA. It wasn't necessary. I was made more than welcome by that charming woman. Who is she?

GASTON. Oh, just my wi . . . why, why she's Huguette. A relative.

CLARA. A nice relative. Gaston?

GASTON. Yes?

CLARA. I have something serious to tell you. I'm not sure how you'll take it.

GASTON. Go ahead, Clara.

CLARA. It's done! I've done it!

GASTON. Done what?

CLARA. I've got my divorce!

GASTON. (*He tries to smile in spite of his dismay. He looks sick and sinks to the octagonal table.*) You have? What wonderful news.

CLARA. So you see, everything I told you this summer was true. I couldn't take a lover until I was legally free from my husband. And now that I am, with a clear conscience I can say: Take me, I'm yours.

GASTON. (*He is tempted, rises, then remembers his wife.*) But surely, Clara, not in here! Come, let's go!

CLARA. Where?

GASTON. Wherever you say. But not here!

CLARA. What's wrong with here?

GASTON. Well, you see I have my . . . my relative in the apartment. Wouldn't it be cozier if we found some out of the way place . . . for just the two of us?

CLARA. And disappoint your nice relative? After she's told me to make myself completely at home . . . in this room, which she's going to do over to suit us?

GASTON. (*Wide-eyed.*) She said that?

CLARA. Yes.

GASTON. Do it over to suit *us?*

CLARA. Yes, just for me and the man I love.

GASTON. How curious. Did she seem well?

CLARA. Quite well. Gaston?

GASTON. Yes, Clara?

CLARA. When I let you bring me here this summer, it was only because I was lonely . . . at loose ends with myself.

GASTON. Well, I tried to tie you together again, the best way I knew how.

CLARA. How I struggled not to give in then and there! (*She straightens his tie.*)

GASTON. (*Terrified his wife may return.*) Yes, you're a very sensual woman.

CLARA. (*Roughly tightening the knot of his tie.*) Intensely sensual! You don't know what it's like for a woman to be both sensual and moral . . . to want to give herself one moment . . . and save herself the next. It's a torture I never want to suffer again!

GASTON. Oh, Clara, you're irresistible! Your eyes, your lips . . .

CLARA. (*Huskily.*) My bags are in the taxi. Fetch them.

GASTON. But . . . you're not thinking of moving in now?

CLARA. Of course I am. You told me you were free, didn't you? When you wanted me to give myself to you? Well, I believed you. And now I'm counting on you! (*She sits on the octagonal table.*)

GASTON. (*Mournfully.*) Oh, good.

CLARA. (*Reassured.*) Yes, isn't it?

GASTON. I'll fetch your bags. (*He doesn't budge.*)

CLARA. What are you waiting for, Gaston?

GASTON. Well, you see, there are times when one is free and then there are other times when one isn't quite so free.

CLARA. Meaning? (*She rises.*)

GASTON. During the summer people go away to escape the hot city . . . women mostly . . . then their husbands . . .

CLARA. Husbands? (*Raising her voice.*) Are you trying to tell me you're a husband? (GASTON *nods.*) A married husband?

GASTON. Don't shout! Please don't shout!

CLARA. It's terrible! You lied to me!

GASTON. I hardly knew you.

CLARA. You deceived me, Gaston. Deceived me! Oh, what am I going to do?

GASTON. I can recommend a hotel . . . on the Place Pigalle. It's on the shady side . . .

CLARA. So that's it! That's your plan. A shady hotel for shady ladies! No! I've never lived in that fashion and I don't intend to start now!

GASTON. Sh! Sh! Calm yourself!

CLARA. Calm myself! For months I've waited for this moment . . . this hour of love's fulfillment. I come to you trembling with desire. I say, 'Take me!' And what do you tell me? 'I'm married, go to Pig Alley!'

GASTON. Clara! Please, Clara!

CLARA. Where's your wife?

GASTON. Here . . . somewhere . . . in the next room, I'm afraid. (*He collapses on the sofa.*)

CLARA. I see . . . it's Huguette! (GASTON *nods.*) But if she's your wife, why did she offer us this room?

GASTON. Are you certain about that, Clara?

CLARA. Certainly I'm certain. She even offered to re-do it.

GASTON. Oh, now I know! (*He rises.*) Don't you see? She mistook you for someone else.

CLARA. Yes. Another of your mistresses.

GASTON. No, not my mistress! Another man's . . .

CLARA. Another . . . Oh! You men! If you had your way, you'd make mistresses of us all!

GASTON. You're right, Clara! (*He tries to pull her out of the room.*) We men are nothing but a bunch of bounders. And you'd be right if you bounded right out of here.

CLARA. Oh no! It's your fault I'm here and I'm staying. (*She sits on the octagonal table.*)

GASTON. But, Clara, don't you see . . . (*He kneels at her side.*) you're rushing us straight into calamity!

CLARA. Who cares? You deserve it.

GASTON. Listen to me, Clara.

CLARA. No! I'm not budging. And that's final!

GASTON. Wait! There is a way out. (*He rises.*) The previous tenant of this apartment asked us to lend him a room to entertain an old girl friend. He's on a sentimental pilgrimage.

CLARA. Are you sure it's not dope?

GASTON. My wife thinks you're this girl. That's why she made you so welcome.

CLARA. Oh, so that was it.

GASTON. Yes. And we won't disillusion her. You'll be this other girl. (*He kneels again at her side.*) It means you can stay here until I find a little place you can call your own.

CLARA. But what about this tenant?

GASTON. I'll arrange everything with him. He's a romantic in love with a dream of yesterday, so he's no threat to you or to me either. Well? What do you say? (*Taking her hand.*) Adultery can still be beautiful inside the home.

CLARA. (*Slapping his hand.*) Gaston!

GASTON. Please, Clara. Please.

CLARA. Well . . . only as a temporary measure . . . until I can think more clearly.

GASTON. Oh, thank you, Clara darling! (CLARA *rises.*)

CLARA. Oh, by the way, what's his name?

GASTON. Whose name?

CLARA. My old lover's. The one you're giving me.

GASTON. Oh, yes. Him. It's Maurice, the Vicomte de Corneblanche.

CLARA. (*Impressed.*) A Vicomte did you say?

GASTON. (*Rushing up the stairs to the boudoir.*) One of the best. A direct descendant of Joan of Arc. Huguette! Huguette! (HUGUETTE *enters from the boudoir.*) Huguette, it's all arranged. Everything's going to work out nicely.

HUGUETTE. (*Coming down the stairs.*) Oh, I'm **so** happy!

GASTON. (*Happily following her down the stairs.*) If you're happy, dear, it makes me even happier. (*He rings for the manservant.*)

HUGUETTE. And to think this charming romance is going to be acted out under our roof! Doesn't it stir a little something in you, Gaston?

GASTON. It certainly does. I can feel the return of summer surging through my blood.

HUGUETTE. (*To* CLARA.) It must give you a funny feeling to be back in this apartment.

CLARA. You have no idea how funny it is. (MAURICE *comes in through the double doors unnoticed.*) For years I've lived to love but one man . . . one man only . . . the Vicomte de Corneblanche. My Maurice!

MAURICE. (*Startled.*) What?

HUGUETTE. Really, Didier!

MAURICE. She said Maurice.

HUGUETTE. And what has that to do with you?

GASTON. Yes, what has that to do with you? Bring in the luggage! I'll take care of the taxi. After you, Madame Gauthier. (GASTON *and* CLARA *go out through the double doors.*)

MAURICE. (*Aside.*) She adores me. This woman adores me! Whoever would have thought it! (*He leaves through the double doors.*)

HUGUETTE. (*Alone, admiring the roses.*) Love! What a beautiful thing is love! (*Unseen by* HUGUETTE, DIDIER *comes in through the French windows. He is carrying an overnight bag.*)

DIDIER. I have returned!

HUGUETTE. Oh! You startled me.

DIDIER. I'm so impatient to see my love again I can't waste time going round to the front door. (HUGUETTE *takes his overnight bag and puts it at the foot of the right stairs.*)

HUGUETTE. Well, monsieur, I'm happy to tell you you won't have long to wait.

DIDIER. What do you mean?

HUGUETTE. The lady you worship is ready to put an end to your torture.

DIDIER. Is that true?

HUGUETTE. I give you my word.

DIDIER. You mean that? Why, it's a miracle! I was afraid it might take more than one night. Ah, madame! Dear, dear madame! (*He takes her hands joyfully.*)

HUGUETTE. She just arrived. Not ten minutes ago.

DIDIER. (*Stunned.*) What's that? She just arrived?

HUGUETTE. Yes.

DIDIER. Who?

HUGUETTE. Who do you think? The lady you shared this apartment with.

DIDIER. The lady I shared . . . ?

HUGUETTE. Yes, and she still loves you.

DIDIER. She still loves me.

HUGUETTE. You look surprised.

DIDIER. Yes! . . . no . . . not really . . . (*All at sea.*) Then she's here? You're quite sure she's here?

HUGUETTE. (*Going to the French windows.*) Yes. She's getting her things from the taxi. (MAURICE *comes through the double doors with two suitcases.*) And there they are.

DIDIER. (*Aside.*) Well, I'll be damned!

HUGUETTE. (*To* MAURICE.) Put them here for the time being. Now I must have a word with the cook.

(*To* DIDIER.) as I hope you'll both have dinner with us tonight.

MAURICE. (*Very much the man of the world.*) Both of us? Tonight? We'd be delighted!

HUGUETTE. (*To* MAURICE.) Didier! Are you completely out of your mind? (*To* DIDIER.) If you'll excuse me . . .

DIDIER. Of course. (HUGUETTE *goes out down the hall.*)

MAURICE. Didier! Guess what's happened to me!

DIDIER. To you? To me!

MAURICE. I'm worshipped by a woman who's never seen me.

DIDIER. And I'm meeting a woman who doesn't exist . . . who was pure imagination on my part!

MAURICE. I knew I was attractive to women but I didn't realize I was that attractive.

DIDIER. You don't think it's an hallucination?

MAURICE. I don't know and I'm not stopping to find out. I should have listened to my Aunt Alice ages ago when she warned me against you.

DIDIER. If you had, you'd be living in some chateau miles from nowhere raising pigs.

MAURICE. Indeed I would. That's why I'm going to Poitou.

DIDIER. To Poitou?

MAURICE. Yes. My Aunt Alice has a rich little orphan picked out for me . . . Rosine Rose . . . and she's been waiting years for me . . . sight unseen . . . for her Prince Charming to bring her to fulfillment.

DIDIER. You poor devil. I can just see your Rosine: straight as a pole; flat as a pancake!

MAURICE. Yes . . . but this pancake is spread with

jam . . . and ready to marry me. And if it weren't **for** you, I'd be in Poitou now . . . fulfilling!

DIDIER. But what about this other woman who worships you?

MAURICE. She'll have to find someone else. I can't go around fulfilling every woman I've never met. (GASTON *comes in through the double doors.*)

GASTON. (*To* MAURICE.) Now then, Didier!

DIDIER. Yes?

GASTON. I said Didier.

DIDIER. Oh, yes. Him. (*To* MAURICE.) Now then, Didier!

MAURICE. What? Who? Oh, that's me.

GASTON. Yes, that's you. There are still two suitcases and a hat box. (*Pause.*) Well, get them!

MAURICE. All right, I'll get them! But you have given me your last order! (*He leaves through the double doors.* GASTON *is furious but gets himself under control.*)

GASTON. (*Approaching a delicate matter.*) Monsieur . . . you'll admit asking me to lend you this room was an unusual request.

DIDIER. Indeed it was.

GASTON. But I granted it, didn't I, without hesitation?

DIDIER. And I'm most grateful.

GASTON. Well, I think this break in routine may amuse my wife.

DIDIER. I do hope so, monsieur.

GASTON. She's not as easy to please as you might think. You have to know how to take her.

DIDIER. I'll try hard, to the best of my ability.

GASTON. Thank you. I can see you're a man I can trust . . . and one good turn deserves another . . .

DIDIER. Oh, absolutely! And the first chance I get, I'll put you on to something good too!

GASTON. That's the idea! I'm going to take you into my confidence.

DIDIER. As you wish, monsieur.

GASTON. I don't want my wife to cheat on me.

DIDIER. (*With mock concern.*) Good Lord, no! You certainly don't.

GASTON. And if you were not here, I'd run that risk.

DIDIER. If I were *not* here?

GASTON. Yes, thanks to you, I may never be a deceived husband.

DIDIER. Well, I certainly didn't come here with the idea of preventing your wife from cheating . . . but go on, I'm listening.

GASTON. To my wife, my middle name is 'Fidelity.' If she knew I was contemplating an affair, she'd take her revenge.

DIDIER. Beat you to the bedpost, as it were.

GASTON. But I have a head start. This summer I brought home a young lady. Nothing happened, unfortunately, but she feels she has an option on me and has come here to pick it up. By a stroke of luck, Huguette has mistaken her for the girl you're expecting.

DIDIER. Ah, I'm beginning to understand.

GASTON. What's more, Clara has agreed to go along with the idea . . . that you be her ex-lover. Of course, when your real love shows up, we may be in a bit of a spot.

DIDIER. Oh, don't let that worry you. We can get around that when the time comes.

GASTON. Then you'll go along with me?

DIDIER. Monsieur, I couldn't refuse you anything and that's a fact!

GASTON. There are too few gentlemen left in this world! I couldn't face having my wife cheat on me first. I'd rather die . . . Quiet! Our women!

DIDIER. Our women? Not yet, Gaston . . . but soon! (*Elbowing him in the ribs.*) Soon! (GASTON *echoes his "soons" and they laugh conspiratorially.* HUGUETTE *and* CLARA *enter through the double doors.*)

HUGUETTE. She's delightful! Gaston, the more you get to know Madame Gauthier, the greater the pleasure.

GASTON. I can well imagine!

HUGUETTE. (*To* CLARA, *and pointing to* DIDIER.) And there he is!

DIDIER. (*He turns, and his voice breaks with emotion.*) Clara!

CLARA. (*With the same over-ripe emotion.*) Maurice!

DIDIER. You! Wonderful you! (*They stagger towards each other like long-lost lovers.*)

CLARA. You! At last! I thought I'd never see you again!

DIDIER. It seemed too much ever to hope for. And now here we are . . . back in our dear old mating place! (*They sit on the hassock, wrapped up in each other.*)

CLARA. The very nest. It makes the heart run wild, doesn't it?

HUGUETTE. (*To* CLARA.) You've had such a long journey, my dear, why don't you make use of my boudoir?

CLARA. (*Without taking her eyes off* DIDIER.) Thank you. I'd love to.

GASTON. (*To* DIDIER.) And why don't you get acquainted with my dressing room? As you're going to be here for a spell, we must all learn to rub along together.

DIDIER. Oh, not all together. Just two at a time.

GASTON. (*To the audience.*) Nice fellow, that.

HUGUETTE. (*Above* CLARA *and* DIDIER, *who are still seated on the hassock.*) Go ahead . . . behave as if we weren't here. Kiss like the lovebirds you used to be.

DIDIER. Shall we, Clara?

CLARA. Why not, Maurice?

DIDIER. (*To* GASTON.) All right with you?

GASTON. (*Suffering.*) How can I stop you? (*He sits on the octagonal table. A long kiss.* HUGUETTE *smiles tenderly.* GASTON *looks over at the kissing couple, then front, several times, in agony as the kiss goes on and on.*) Is it nice?

DIDIER. Delicious! You have no idea! Simply delicious! Another!

GASTON. (*Sharply.*) No more! (*He rises.*)

HUGUETTE. (*Pushing* GASTON *back down.*) But of course, more! More! We love it! (*Snuggling* GASTON.) Don't we, Gaston? (GASTON *groans.* DIDIER *and* CLARA *resume their kissing.* HUGUETTE *looks at* GASTON, *who manages to smile.*)

CLARA. You kiss as divinely as ever. (*They resume their kissing.*)

HUGUETTE. (*To* GASTON.) Love can be so beautiful!

GASTON. (*Rises; to* DIDIER, *annoyed.*) When you're ready!

HUGUETTE. (*To* CLARA.) This way, my dear.

CLARA. (*Woozy from the kissing.*) I won't be long, Maurice, dearest! (HUGUETTE *and* CLARA *go up the stairs.*)

DIDIER. (*Rises.*) Hurry back, you lovely darling!

HUGUETTE. And here is the door. But how foolish of me. You must know every inch around here.

CLARA. I thought I did. But I'm not quite myself. (CLARA *and* HUGUETTE *go into the boudoir.* DIDIER *starts up the right stairs after them.*)

GASTON. (*Rushing up the left stairs; to* DIDIER.) And we go this way, if you don't mind.

DIDIER. (*Outside the bedroom door.*) Some girl, this Clara of ours.

GASTON. (*Annoyed.*) Ours!

DIDIER. On the surface, I mean. Ours on the surface. And some surface, I might add. Fine frame, silken hair, bountiful breasts.

GASTON. (*Eagerly.*) Are they? Are they really bountiful?

DIDIER. Firm and round. As firm and round as the logs you sell.

GASTON. (*Impressed.*) As good as that, hm? Still, you can't throw them on a fire on a cold day.

DIDIER. Well, *I* wouldn't.

GASTON. You took your part quite well.

DIDIER. Oh, that was nothing. I can do much better. (*He heads for the boudoir.*)

GASTON. (*Stopping him.*) Stop! What you did was good enough! (*They go into the bedroom as* MAURICE *shows in an enchanting girl of about twenty.*)

MAURICE. Mademoiselle . . . if you will come this way . . .

GIRL. Is Madame Dubois at home?

MAURICE. Yes. But I'm afraid she has guests.

GIRL. I must see her. It's most important.

MAURICE. I'll tell her you're here. If you would be so good as to wait in the adjoining room . . . (**With** *the disdain of a superior manservant.*) this one **has** been loaned out.

GIRL. Very well.

MAURICE. Who shall I say is calling?

GIRL. Mademoiselle Rosine Rose.

MAURICE. (*Thunderstruck.*)   Rosine!   But   **I** thought . . .

ROSINE. Yes?

MAURICE. Nothing. You said your name was . . .

ROSINE. Rosine Rose. And don't be afraid to disturb Madame Dubois . . . she's a close friend of the family. (*She goes into the study.*)

MAURICE. (*In shock.*) No! Impossible! Not Rosine! Not my Rosine! (DIDIER *re-enters and comes down the stairs for his suitcase.*) Didier! Guess what's happened now . . . guess what's happened to me!

DIDIER. To you? To me! It's fabulous!

MAURICE. It's frightful! Another girl has just arrived. (DIDIER *does a "take."*)

DIDIER. Another girl?

MAURICE. It's her! My Rosine. My millions have arrived!

DIDIER. No!

MAURICE. Yes! They just walked through that **door.** And I can't collect because you installed me as **a** servant to friends of her family. What am I going **to** do?

DIDIER. I can't stop to tell you now. Gaston has **just** thrown Clara into my arms.

MAURICE. Clara?

DIDIER. She's dynamite!

MAURICE. But Huguette?

DIDIER. She's a time bomb!

MAURICE. (*Plaintively.*) Yes, but what about my Rosine?

DIDIER. I'll tell you later, Maurice. After I light her fuse! (*Laughing, he goes into the bedroom with his suitcase.* MAURICE, *stunned, turns to the audience.*)

BLACKOUT

CURTAIN

ACT TWO

Scene: *The same.*

Time: *A few minutes only have elapsed since Act One.*

As the curtain rises, Huguette *is chatting with an agitated* Rosine Rose.

Huguette. Then your guardian doesn't know you're here?

Rosine. No. Last night I had words with him so I decided to come to Paris.

Huguette. Oh? You and your guardian don't get on well?

Rosine. No. All I hear is 'mustn't.' Mustn't do this, Rosine. Mustn't do that, Rosine. Mustn't, mustn't, mustn't, Rosine. Oh, Huguette, I had to get away.

Huguette. But without telling anyone? Rosine, do you realize what you've done?

Rosine. I don't care what I've done!

Huguette. But aren't you about to be engaged?

Rosine. For nineteen years I've been about to be engaged. We have a friend, Alice de la Granville, and while I was still in the cradle, she and my guardian decided I should marry her nephew.

Huguette. Don't you like him? (Maurice *comes in from the hall. As an excuse to eavesdrop, he dusts around with a feather duster.*)

37

ROSINE. I don't know. I've never seen him. He lives in Paris and has never made the slightest attempt to know me. Not even yesterday, my twentieth birthday. And he was sent a special invitation to the party.

HUGUETTE. Perhaps he was unavoidably detained. (MAURICE *nods in agreement.*)

ROSINE. For nineteen years? He's no good. He's unstable and he's mean. (MAURICE's *face drops.*) He thinks nothing of making a fool of me so I'm going to strike back . . . take a lover!

MAURICE. (*Mournfully.*) Oh!

HUGUETTE. I trust our conversation interests you?

MAURICE. Oh, it does!

HUGUETTE. Really!

MAURICE. Honest and truly! (*Aside.*) Cheating on me! And before we're married! Oh! (*He dusts the doorway and enters the study.*)

HUGUETTE. (*Sits on the sofa.*) Take a lover? Who?

ROSINE. It doesn't matter. I'll settle for the first man I meet. (*Seated on the sofa.*) Do you know the moment I left the station I went straight up to a man. I accosted him on the street.

HUGUETTE. What?

ROSINE. I said, 'Take me home with you. I want to punish my fiance.'

HUGUETTE. And what did he say?

ROSINE. 'I'm terribly sorry, mademoiselle, but I have a wife, a mistress and, at the moment, I'm obliging my secretary.'

HUGUETTE. The men in Paris are awfully busy. (GASTON *comes in from the hall, a telegram in his hand.*) Oh, Gaston. (*She rises.*)

ROSINE. (*Rising.*) Hello, Monsieur Dubois.

GASTON. (*Not recognizing her.*) Mademoiselle?

HUGUETTE. Oh, Gaston, don't you remember Rosine? She was one of my bridesmaids.

GASTON. Of course, I remember you. I could hardly take my eyes off you on my wedding day!

HUGUETTE. (*With a playful pout.*) And me? You didn't look at me at all?

GASTON. Well, I had every reason to believe I'd be seeing more of you later. (*He starts for the stairs.*)

HUGUETTE. Gaston! Rosine is in Paris for a few days. I don't want her to go to a hotel so I'm putting her up here.

GASTON. Here?

HUGUETTE. Any reason we can't?

GASTON. What? Oh no, darling. (*To* ROSINE.) Delighted to have you. The more the merrier. Will you excuse me? A telegram for one of our guests. (*He goes into the bedroom.*)

ROSINE. Oh? You have other guests?

HUGUETTE. Yes, a true love story. (*She rings the bell.*) I'll tell you all about it. (MAURICE *comes in.*)

MAURICE. (*Gloomily.*) Madame rang?

HUGUETTE. Before you pack your things, bring in mademoiselle's suitcase.

MAURICE. What? Mademoiselle is staying here?

HUGUETTE. What has that to do with you? Come along, Rosine. I've never had such an insufferable servant.

ROSINE. Yes, he is insufferable. (*They go into the boudoir.*)

MAURICE. Insufferable? Me? Irresistible me insufferable? (DIDIER *comes in swiftly from the bedroom.*)

DIDIER. Maurice! Maurice!

MAURICE. What is it?

DIDIER. A catastrophe!

MAURICE. For whom?

DIDIER. For me.

MAURICE. Good news at last!

DIDIER. You're involved too!

MAURICE. (*His face drops.*) Oh!

DIDIER. (*Handing* MAURICE *the open telegram.*) It's from your Aunt Alice de la Granville.

MAURICE. So now you're reading my telegrams!

DIDIER. It was given to me. After all, I am Maurice de Corneblanche!

MAURICE. (*Reads the telegram.*) Oh, my God! I gave Aunt Alice this address but I never dreamed she'd look me up.

DIDIER. And she's already here in Paris!

MAURICE. Yes, searching for my Rosine . . .

DIDIER. And when your Aunt Alice descends on this apartment, she'll know I'm not her precious Maurice and I'll be shown the door just as I was set to spend the night!

MAURICE. What about me? Operating as a servant right under Auntie's nose. I'll be disinherited.

DIDIER. Wait! Everything can still be all right!

MAURICE. How?

DIDIER. Disappear.

MAURICE. Disappear?

DIDIER. You wanted to leave, didn't you? Well, go!

MAURICE. No. I can't now.

DIDIER. Can't? Why?

MAURICE. Rosine is going to stay here. She's out for revenge. I can't let her out of my sight!

DIDIER. Then you're not going to leave?

MAURICE. No! Everything's changed. When that doorbell rings, you'll answer it!

DIDIER. Me?

MAURICE. Yes, you. My Aunt Alice expects to see me as a guest.

DIDIER. But what about me . . . parading around as a servant?

MAURICE. You created this mess. Clean it up! (HUGUETTE *comes in from the boudoir.*)

HUGUETTE. Didier?

DIDIER. Yes, madame?

HUGUETTE. (*Amazed.*) What?

DIDIER. Oh! (*To* MAURICE.) Didier!

MAURICE. Madame?

HUGUETTE. Will you bring in mademoiselle's suitcase or must I ask you again?

DIDIER. Do as you're told! You seem to have no idea how to go about your work!

MAURICE. I look forward to getting some pointers from you, monsieur, later. (*He goes out down the hall.*)

HUGUETTE. Do you know I can't stop thinking about your bedroom?

DIDIER. How exciting!

HUGUETTE. Are you going to change all the furniture?

DIDIER. Yes. And here, in the center of the room, will be our bed.

HUGUETTE. Our bed?

DIDIER. Yes, ours. Since this is your apartment, it's really your bed too.

HUGUETTE. Will there be a pouffe somewhere in the room?

DIDIER. Of course. And there I'll sit . . . fondling my darling.

HUGUETTE. You're making it sound like the room of my dreams.

DIDIER. Yes, that's it. A room in which to dream. But never to sleep.

HUGUETTE. How heavenly! To dream but never to sleep. Now I sleep and sleep and sleep . . . (*She sits on the sofa.*)

DIDIER. Doesn't your husband ever wake you up?

HUGUETTE. Oh no. That would defeat the purpose of the Ovaltine he takes.

DIDIER. Madame . . . it would serve your husband right if you looked around for someone . . . not quite so sleepy. (*He sits next to her.*)

HUGUETTE. No, never. Unless I were to discover he had deceived me. Then I'd feel it my duty to retaliate. But since there's no question of that . . .

DIDIER. No, no question at all. But it troubles me to see that shadow of sadness in your eyes. Madame, you've been so kind I'd like to share my happiness with you! (*He leans her back into the corner of the sofa.*)

HUGUETTE. That would be nice. I'm thrilled already with the idea of helping you re-live those memorable hours.

DIDIER. (*Urgently.*) But what about the present? The present can have some electric moments too. (*The doorbell rings loudly. Their faces snap front.*)

HUGUETTE. Oh, if you only knew what it's like for me to hear two hearts . . . the hearts of two strangers . . . vibrating . . . vibrating . . . all around me. (*He has her trapped in the corner of the sofa. The doorbell rings again. He listens anxiously, aware* MAURICE *expects him to answer the door.*)

DIDIER. Yes, I hear the vibrations. All too clearly!

HUGUETTE. Pay no attention. Didier takes hours to answer the door. Now where were we?

DIDIER. In the bedroom.

HUGUETTE. Oh yes. On the pouffe. (*The doorbell rings again.*)

DIDIER. We'll have to pick it up later. (*He abruptly moves away from her.*) I'll be back! (*He rushes out through the double doors.*)

HUGUETTE. (*Astonished.*) What on earth's come over him? (*At this moment,* CLARA *comes in from the boudoir, fleeing from* GASTON, *who is in hot pursuit. He is holding the hem of her skirt. She races down the right stairs.*)

CLARA. Oh! No! No! Not that, please! (*She stops dead in her running position at the sight of* HUGUETTE. GASTON *drops her skirt and holds his hand out, immobile, at his side.* HUGUETTE *half rises from the sofa to see what is going on.*) Oh! You! Madame! . . . Your husband. He's so kind. He was just trying to give me a hand. (*Her face drops as she realizes what she's said.* GASTON *puts his "guilty" outstretched hand behind his back.* DIDIER *re-enters, carrying a small package.*)

HUGUETTE. Who was it, monsieur? (*She rises.*)

DIDIER. Only the delivery boy. I believe he said it's Ovaltine. (*He looks meaningfully at* HUGUETTE.)

GASTON. You answered the door?

DIDIER. Oh. Yes. Habit. (*To* CLARA.) You see, Clara, the doorbell rings and I rush to answer it.

CLARA. Oh, Maurice. All your old habits are coming back! (*Rushing into* DIDIER's *arms.*) Oh, my love! How did I ever live without you?

GASTON. (*To* HUGUETTE.) Look at them! Does it remind you of anything?

HUGUETTE. (*With a look at* GASTON.) No, not really! (*She brusquely goes out down the hall.* GASTON *follows her up to the archway.* DIDIER *is kissing*

CLARA's *neck, while she sighs appreciatively and looks heavenwards.*)

GASTON. (*Coming back.*) She's gone. (*They don't stop kissing.*) I said, 'She's gone.'

DIDIER. Who?

GASTON. My wife. I don't understand it. Something seems to happen to her every time you two start kissing.

CLARA. Oh, Gaston, you've put me in a terrible position. If only I'd known you were married!

GASTON. Under certain circumstances it's difficult for a woman to distinguish between a married man and a bachelor.

CLARA. But we never reached those circumstances! Oh, how I envy those medieval women who were given the means of protecting themselves from their own weakness!

GASTON. (*Very jealous.*) Let me tell you, if I could lay my hands on one of those medieval items, I'd put you right under lock and key . . . (*Taking her in his arms.*) because I want to keep you safe and chaste for me. I could become insanely jealous if . . . (*He stops and listens.*) Listen! My wife! She's coming back. (*To* DIDIER.) Quick! Grab her! (*He hurls* DIDIER *and* CLARA *into each other's arms and pushes them on to the hassock.*) Hold her tight! Don't move! (CLARA *and* DIDIER *freeze.* GASTON, *near the double doors, listens in the dead silence.*) Ah, she went the other way. (*He sees* CLARA's *head sliding on to* DIDIER's *shoulder.*)

CLARA. (*After a long and loving sigh.*) Oh, Maurice!

GASTON. What is it, Clara? Is he doing something he shouldn't?

CLARA. He's not but you are! Gaston, you're mak-

ing a nervous wreck of me. You kiss me and you
caress me, then push me into another man's arms . . .
(*Her voice melts provocatively.*) although, I must say,
he's doing rather nicely.

DIDIER. Thank you, madame. You're very kind. (*He
rises and makes way for* GASTON *to take over his
embrace.*) Your turn, monsieur. That's the idea, isn't
it?

GASTON. Yes! That's the idea! (*He sits on the spot
vacated by* DIDIER *and makes a grab for* CLARA, *but
she rises and* GASTON *sprawls over the hassock.*)

CLARA. No! No, I can't stand any more! It's too
much! From this man to that man, from that man to
this man! I think I'm going to faint!

GASTON. (*Rises.*) Not now! Please, not now! . . .
I'll be alone with you tonight, I promise.

CLARA. (*Slumped against* GASTON.) And will you
promise that we will go to bed early?

GASTON. The earlier the better. (*He starts to cuddle*
CLARA.)

DIDIER. Monsieur, there's someone . . .

GASTON. (*Alarmed.*) . . . coming?! (*He pushes*
CLARA *away and starts shaking her hand.* ROSINE
comes in from the boudoir. GASTON, *with an effort to
appear natural.*) Yes, I'm acquainted with all the
European timbers. The Polish trunk is superior to the
Yugoslav. Still our own native trunk is . . .

DIDIER. (*Eyeing* ROSINE *appreciatively from the
foot of the stairs.*) Superb!

GASTON. (*Looking up at* ROSINE.) Yes, not bad at
all. (CLARA *hits* GASTON *on the back.*)

ROSINE. I think I left something in here. I do hope
I haven't interrupted anything.

GASTON. No, dear. I was about to take Madame

Gauthier into the dining room. She's famished. Aren't
you, Clara? (*He starts leading* CLARA *to the study.*)

CLARA. No, not in the least.

GASTON. (*Winking at* CLARA *and speaking author-
itatively.*) Oh, yes you are! You're famished. I can
see you are. A glass of port . . . some biscuits . . .

CLARA. But I tell you I'm not hungry!

ROSINE. But I am, Monsieur Dubois! I'm starving!

GASTON. You are?

ROSINE. I haven't eaten all day.

GASTON. You haven't? Oh, you're just saying that
to be polite. You're not hungry at all. And I won't
force you. You just get on with what you came in for.
(*He returns to* CLARA *at the study door.*)

DIDIER. Monsieur! Don't forget this. (*He holds up
the package.*)

CLARA. What is it?

DIDIER. His Ovaltine.

CLARA. Ovaltine? And port wine? What kind of
drink is that?

GASTON. It's a new cocktail! (GASTON *and* CLARA
go into the study.)

ROSINE. Ovaltine and port wine? It sounds horrible.

DIDIER. It will do him good, madame.

ROSINE. (*Correcting him.*) Mademoiselle.

DIDIER. Mademoiselle. Oh, you must be the visitor
from Poitou.

ROSINE. I suppose a Parisian can always tell someone fresh from the provinces.

DIDIER. (*Gazing at her.*) But the provinces have
their own attractions.

ROSINE. Yes, particularly if you live in Paris.

DIDIER. I can see you intend to make the most of
your stay.

ROSINE. I'm going out very night.

DIDIER. With your charming hostess?

ROSINE. No doubt. But the places I want to see, two women alone are not likely to get very far.

DIDIER. Well, if I might be of service . . .

ROSINE. When?

DIDIER. Whenever you say.

ROSINE. I say now.

DIDIER. Now!

ROSINE. Yes. I'm hungry. We'll have a pancake then go to a play.

DIDIER. The two of us?

ROSINE. Why not? Huguette's so busy and you're so free! (MAURICE *comes in through the double doors carrying a suitcase.*) Ah, my bag. Thank you. I'll take it. (*She goes to the right stairs, then turns back to* DIDIER.) On second thought, after we eat, I'd rather go dancing!

MAURICE. Huh?

ROSINE. Give me a chance to change and I'll be yours for the evening! You won't regret it! (*She goes happily into the boudoir.*)

MAURICE. You're dating my Rosine?

DIDIER. No, she's dating me.

MAURICE. Out of spite.

DIDIER. Look. It's not Rosine I want. Huguette gets top priority.

MAURICE. Then promise me you will make Rosine hate you!

DIDIER. If that's what you want, I promise.

MAURICE. Make her see how despicable you are!

DIDIER. But to everyone around here I'm Maurice de Corneblanche. Just how much do you want me to blacken your name?

MAURICE. The name doesn't matter; it's the person. To save Rosine for me, you have my permission to blacken my name! (HUGUETTE *comes in from the hall.*)

HUGUETTE. (*To* MAURICE.) Oh, Didier . . . have you seen Monsieur Dubois?

DIDIER. I think he's in the study.

HUGUETTE. (*Going towards the study.*) I must speak to him. (*To* MAURICE, *as she passes him.*) About you, actually.

DIDIER. (*Quickly stopping her.*) Oh, let me! I'll get him for you. (*He goes to the study door, listens, knocks.*) Hello in there! Monsieur Dubois! Coucou! (*He knocks again.*) Coucou! Here I come! (*He knocks again.*)

HUGUETTE. (*Startled.*) But my dear Monsieur de Corneblanche, there's no need for you to knock.

DIDIER. Oh! No . . . I know . . . only my Clara is in there too. And whenever she sees me unexpectedly she gets all undone, so I give her a chance to pull herself together. I call out, 'Coucou! Here I come!'

HUGUETTE. Oh, I see. (GASTON *comes in completely dishevelled: hair mussed, coat open, tie pulled half way down his shirt.*)

GASTON. (*Between clenched teeth.*) I can't even study my logs without somebody . . . (*He sees* HUGUETTE.) Ah, it's you, darling!

HUGUETTE. Gaston, what have you been doing?

GASTON. Me? Oh . . . I was fooling around in there . . . with a new cocktail . . . shaking it up . . . so naturally . . . (*He pantomimes a violent shaking of a cocktail, making his hair fly. He laughs.* DIDIER *joins in.* MAURICE *roars with laughter.*)

HUGUETTE. (*To* MAURICE.) There you go again!

Gaston, you simply must ring up the agency and get someone to replace Didier.

MAURICE. I'm sorry. I apologize, madame.

HUGUETTE. A bit late in the day, I'm afraid.

MAURICE. But I like it here! I'll give up my radio, stereo, color TV!

GASTON. Well, that's something.

HUGUETTE. Dismiss him, Gaston! Dismiss him! (*She goes up the stairs.*)

DIDIER. (*To* HUGUETTE.) Is there anything *I* can do for you, madame?

HUGUETTE. (*A bit perturbed.*) Thank you. I mean, not right this minute. (*She goes into the bedroom.*)

GASTON. (*To* MAURICE, *as he takes some money from his pocket.*) Here's a week's wages. Now clear out!

MAURICE. Very good, monsieur. (*He takes off his apron and behind* GASTON's *back, flings it at* DIDIER, *who catches it.*) And who shall I see about the bonus?

GASTON. (*Turning back from his progress towards the study.*) What bonus?

MAURICE. (*Who is now only in pants and shirt.*) The bonus you promised me for the cigarette case with the name 'Clara' engraved on it. I should like the money before I leave.

GASTON. Who said anything about your leaving? No. There's just one thing I ask: in future, perform your duties quietly and discreetly.

MAURICE. That's the least I can do.

GASTON. With diligence and dispatch.

MAURICE. You may depend on me, monsieur. (*As* GASTON *starts for the study, the doorbell rings.*)

GASTON. Didier . . . the doorbell.

MAURICE. That's right. The doorbell. (*The doorbell rings again.*)

GASTON. Well . . . what are you waiting for?

MAURICE. (*Who has not moved an inch.*) What? What do you mean?

GASTON. The door . . . answer it . . . with diligence and dispatch!

MAURICE. (*Still immobile.*) I can't think what I'm waiting for! Why don't I go? (*He throws an urgent, desperate look to* DIDIER.)

DIDIER. (*Hiding the apron from* GASTON *and moving quickly towards the double doors.*) Don't disturb Didier. Finish your talk.

GASTON. (*Astonished, to* DIDIER.) But I can't allow you to answer . . .

DIDIER. It's nothing! It's like old times! (*He goes out.*)

GASTON. That fellow has me baffled. (*Confidentially.*) Didier . . .

MAURICE. Monsieur?

GASTON. I need someone I can trust to keep an eye on this Maurice de Corneblanche.

MAURICE. That's the job for me! If I catch him twisting his way around that sweet young girl . . .

GASTON. Never mind the girl. It's Clara who interests me. Look after Clara. Understand? (*He starts for the study.*)

MAURICE. Yes, perfectly. I'll keep an eye on her.

GASTON. Never leave her alone with him!

MAURICE. I'll never leave her alone with anybody!

GASTON. Stay close to her all the time.

MAURICE. Morning, noon and night.

GASTON. That's it. You're going to be her chastity belt . . . always around, always respectful! (*He goes into the study.* DIDIER *pops his head in through the double doors. Seeing* MAURICE *is alone, He comes in swiftly. He is wearing the apron.*)

DIDIER. Maurice! Maurice!

MAURICE. (*Almost swooning.*) Oh, if you only knew what I've just been turned into!

DIDIER. What?

MAURICE. A chastity belt! A living chastity belt! I never thought I'd sink that low!

DIDIER. Well, gird your strength. Your aunt's here!

MAURICE. Aunt Alice! Here! I'm done! (*He darts here and there in panic.*)

DIDIER. I'm bringing her in. I can't leave her to rot in the hall.

MAURICE. What if someone comes in and finds me with her?

DIDIER. Get rid of her as fast as you can! (*He, too, is in a panic.*) And don't panic! That's the only way out of this! We mustn't panic!

MAURICE. No. We mustn't panic!

DIDIER. I'll keep guard. You sit down quietly . . . (*He shoves* MAURICE *into the sofa.*) and don't forget you're a guest in this apartment! And take off those white gloves!

MAURICE. And if they see you wearing that apron?

DIDIER. I'll put on my overcoat. Now don't worry. I'll stop anybody from coming in. I'll watch them all . . . dash from door to door to door . . . (*He goes out through the double doors.*)

MAURICE. That's the way! Watch the doors and dash them all! (*He takes off his gloves and puts them in his pocket.*) No, we mustn't panic! We mustn't panic! (*As he hears* DIDIER *re-entering, he hides behind the sofa.* DIDIER *invites* AUNT ALICE *into the room. She is as stern-faced and as haughty as it is possible to go on being nowadays.*)

DIDIER. Would mademoiselle be so kind as to come this way?

ALICE. Of course mademoiselle would. I didn't travel all those miles to loiter in a hallway.

DIDIER. No, I don't suppose you did. (*He puts down her Gladstone bag near the door.*)

ALICE. Where's my nephew?

DIDIER. Yes. Where is he?

ALICE. Well, call him! Maurice!

MAURICE. (*Popping up from behind the sofa.*) Looking for me, auntie?

ALICE. No. I'm looking for her. Where is she?

MAURICE. (*To* DIDIER.) Where is she?

DIDIER. (*To* MAURICE.) Who?

MAURICE. (*To* ALICE.) Who?

ALICE. Stop acting like an idiot and tell me where I can find her! (*To* DIDIER.) You there! Butler! Aren't you wanted in the pantry? (*She hands him her umbrella.*)

DIDIER. I'll go and see, mademoiselle, and report right back. (*He places the umbrella near the fireplace and goes out through the double doors.*)

ALICE. Do you realize Rosine ran away because of you?

MAURICE. (*Acting the innocent.*) No! How awful! Where did she run to?

ALICE. That's what I'm asking you.

MAURICE. (*The same.*) You don't know?

ALICE. As usual, you're useless! You know nothing! (*Attacking.*) What are you doing in shirtsleeves at this hour?

MAURICE. In shirtsleeves? Oh, yes, I hadn't noticed!

ALICE. You've only just got up!

MAURICE. Oh no!

ALICE. Disgraceful!

MAURICE. It's because . . . it's because of the heat.

ALICE. The heat?

MAURICE. Yes, it's unbearable in here. The radiators are boiling hot.

ALICE. That's strange. I hadn't noticed it. But now that you mention it . . . help me off with my coat.

MAURICE. Why bother if you're only staying a few minutes?

ALICE. A few minutes? I'm here to find Rosine for as long as it takes. I have my whole life ahead of me.

MAURICE. I'm so glad to hear it.

ALICE. But you're right. The heat is overpowering. I shall be overcome. A fine thing that would be! (MAURICE *sees* DIDIER *enter from the hall. He is wearing an overcoat, with the collar turned up, over his apron.* DIDIER *starts to creep across the room to the study in order to listen at the door and stop anyone from coming in.*) Well, are you going to help me off with my coat?

MAURICE. (*In panic.*) Yes, yes, I'll help you, auntie! (MAURICE *spins* ALICE *round so she will not be facing* DIDIER. *But as her coat comes off, she spins around on her own axis and sees* DIDIER *creeping up to the study door. She watches him until he gets to the keyhole.*)

ALICE. What's that butler up to! Peeking through keyholes!

DIDIER. Not peeking, mademoiselle. Listening.

ALICE. Are you going out?

DIDIER. No, coming in.

ALICE. With an overcoat on? Where I come from it's customary to put on a coat when you *leave* the house.

DIDIER. I'm rather delicate. It's freezing cold in this apartment.

ALICE. What?

DIDIER. I said it's freezing cold in this apartment. (DIDIER *does not understand* MAURICE *who, behind* ALICE'S *back, is gesturing that it's hot not cold.*)

ALICE. What a bag of nonsense! You mean to tell me . . .

DIDIER. The central heating's broken down. The radiators are like ice.

MAURICE. (*Flapping his shirt against his chest.*) I'm stifling!

DIDIER. (*Buttoning his coat collar.*) I'm shivering! (DIDIER *and* MAURICE *shout across* ALICE.)

MAURICE. Stifling!

DIDIER. Shivering!

ALICE. Is it freezing cold or boiling hot in here, that's what I want to know! Between the two of you, I feel I'm standing in a draught! (*Sneezes.*) Atchoo!

MAURICE. Here! Put on your coat! (*He flings her coat around her.*)

DIDIER. (*Wrapping her scarf around her neck many times.*) Yes, and your scarf! Don't you dare catch cold!

ALICE. Very amusing, these schoolboy pranks . . . hot and cold, cold and hot! But I'm telling you, Maurice, if I get pneumonia, you'll be disinherited!

MAURICE. Come, come, auntie-tauntie, with your lungs?

DIDIER. (*Rushing to pick up her Gladstone bag.*) Would mademoiselle like me to call a taxi?

MAURICE. A good idea! Off you go! (*He rushes* ALICE *towards the double doors.*)

ALICE. (*To* DIDIER.) Put down my bag! If it's a

question of one of us showing the other the door, I'm the one who's doing the showing. (*Forcefully.*) **Get** out of my sight! (DIDIER *puts down her bag and goes out down the hall.*) What a clod that man is! **Now** that we're finally by ourselves, you can stop treating me like a half-wit hayseed from Poitou. Whose apartment is this?

MAURICE. (*Thinking fast.*) It . . . it belongs to friends of your nephew Antoine.

ALICE. And you're staying with them for awhile?

MAURICE. Yes.

ALICE. If they're Antoine's friends, it makes me feel more at home. (*She sits in the right chair.*) Now listen carefully to what I have to say.

MAURICE. Yes, but . . .

ALICE. Quiet! (MAURICE *sits on the hassock.*) Do you know why I left the pigs and the chateau behind to come here?

MAURICE. (*Half-rising.*) Yes, but . . .

ALICE. Quiet! (*He sits.*) To find your fiancee, certainly! But there's another reason, my boy. I'm giving you six weeks in which to get married.

MAURICE. (*Half-rising.*) Six weeks, but . . .

ALICE. Will you be quiet! (*He sits.*) If you aren't married by then, your allowance will cease, your staff of life cut off at the source! You have been warned! (DIDIER *comes tiptoeing back into the room.* MAURICE *rises, again trying to prevent* ALICE *from spotting him. This time* DIDIER *prowls around the bedroom and boudoir doors.*)

MAURICE. All right. I'll do as you say. (*He pats her fondly to stop her from turning around and seeing* DIDIER.) What rosy cheeks my sweet auntie-tauntie has!

ALICE. Stop playing with my cheeks. I'm not a baby! (*She rises.*)

MAURICE. If you say so. (*He rushes her to the archway.*) Now home you go, back to Poitou with your mind at ease.

ALICE. (*Irritated.*) You know perfectly well I can't go back without Rosine!

MAURICE. Why not?

ALICE. (*Shouting.*) Because it's my duty to take her back to her guardian! (DIDIER *signals* MAURICE *to keep his aunt quiet.*)

MAURICE. Please! Not so loud!

ALICE. (*Shouting louder.*) I shall speak as loudly as I choose!

MAURICE. (*Almost whispering.*) Someone is trying to sleep.

ALICE. At this hour?

MAURICE. Yes. Someone who's afraid to sleep at night because of the dark.

ALICE. Oh, I see. Poor soul.

MAURICE. So let's speak softly, ever so softly, shall we?

ALICE. (*In a voice as low as his.*) Yes. Ever so softly. Not a sound!

MAURICE. (*A whisper.*) That's it. Not a sound. (*At this moment,* DIDIER *hangs on with all his might to the handle of the bedroom door, about to open, and the railing. He yells fiercely to the great alarm of* ALICE, *who turns and sees him.*)

DIDIER. No! No! No! You can't come in!

ALICE. (*Starting towards* DIDIER.) What's he doing back? (DIDIER *hangs on desperately to the doorknob and the railing.*)

DIDIER. (*Still shouting.*) Please, madame! One moment! I beg you!

VOICE OF HUGUETTE. (*From behind the door.*) But why can't I come in?

DIDIER. (*His voice ringing with pathos.*) I'm with my beloved! Locked in her arms!

ALICE. (*Stepping back frightened.*) His beloved! The man's deranged!

DIDIER. Go away! I beg you, go away!

VOICE OF HUGUETTE. Oh, very well!

DIDIER. (*At the top of his voice.*) Thank you! (*His overcoat has slipped off his shoulders during his struggle with the doorknob. He is relieved the crisis is over.*) Oh God! (*He comes down the left stairs, facing the audience. He is worn out, his hair dishevelled, breathless. He looks at* ALICE, *who stares back at him as if he is insane.*)

ALICE. (*Using a voice reserved for mental cases.*) Are you feeling better now, my man? Aren't you ashamed to have made such a noise? It was very naughty. You could easily have awakened the poor soul who's trying to sleep.

DIDIER. (*In his natural voice.*) What poor soul? Nobody in his right mind would try to sleep at this hour!

ALICE. (*Her head swivels to* MAURICE.) Well, Maurice?

MAURICE. (*Rushing up the right stairs.*) Of course someone is trying to sleep! You know as well as I do . . . you know . . . you know the one . . .

DIDIER. (*Realizing he is supposed to agree.*) Oh! Yes! Of course! (*He puts his finger to his lips. To* ALICE, *sharp and clear.*) Shh! Shh! (*Lowering his voice.*) We must be as quiet as mice . . . because of the one . . . who is trying to sleep. (*He has started to tiptoe up the left stairs.*)

MAURICE. (*On the platform, making the same gestures.*) Shh! Shh!

DIDIER. (*Turning to* ALICE.) Shh! Shh!

ALICE. (*Alarmed; to the audience.*) I've dropped into a branch of the lunatic asylum!

DIDIER. I'm carrying out orders.

MAURICE. Yes. She gave him instructions to shout what he shouted. (*He comes down the right stairs.*)

DIDIER. (*Following* MAURICE *down the stairs.*) At three forty-seven.

MAURICE. (*Looking at his watch.*) Forty-eight. (*He shows it to* ALICE.) He's right on time!

ALICE. Then the lady of the house is also . . . (*Pantomiming screwy.*) round the bend?

DIDIER. Remember! (*As he tiptoes past* ALICE, *his finger to his lips.*) Shh! Shh! Not a sound! Because of the one . . . who is trying to sleep! (*He heads towards the hall.*)

MAURICE. (*Following* DIDIER *with exactly the same movements.*) Shh! Shh!

DIDIER. (*The same.*) Shh! Shh! (ALICE *is caught up and copies them.*)

ALICE. Shh! Shh! (DIDIER *goes out down the hall.* ALICE *stops suddenly in the middle of a tiptoe.*) *Maurice!* (MAURICE *stops dead in his tracks.*) Who's crazy around here? You? Your friends? Or the butler?

MAURICE. I don't really know. We're so used to each other we pay no attention.

ALICE. I see, you're all affected! But I didn't come here to nurse a pack of ninnies. I've two or three addresses where Rosine might be. I'm going to try them! (*She goes towards the archway.*)

MAURICE. (*Following her.*) Oh, yes! Hurry before she slips through your fingers!

ALICE. I shall return at nine, after dinner.

MAURICE. To Poitou?

ALICE. No. Here. (*She comes back down into the room.*)

MAURICE. Here?. But auntie, this isn't my home.

ALICE. Antoine's friends are my friends. I'm not fussy. (*Looking around the room.*) A cot in a corner somewhere will do. Fix it up, and don't forget my last will and testament.

MAURICE. (*Mechanically.*) It's never out of my mind.

ALICE. (*Ironically.*) Really?

MAURICE. I mean you're constantly in my thoughts. (*He mops his brow.*) In this terrible heat, you'd be frightfully uncomfortable here. Look at me. Wringing wet.

ALICE. Maurice . . . what kind of handkerchief is that? (*He sees the white glove he has pulled from his pocket instead of a handkerchief.*)

MAURICE. (*Confused for a moment.*) Oh, it's . . . (*With assurance.*) A handkerchief. A white handkerchief.

ALICE. It looks like a glove!

MAURICE. Yes, it looks like a glove but it's a handkerchief. The latest thing. All the rage. Of course, it must seem odd to someone out of the swim. Ha-ha-ha.

ALICE. Yes, I must be out of the swim. (*Imitating* MAURICE.) Ha-ha-ha. (*To the audience.*) There's something infernally odd going on in Paris. Well, no matter. (*She looks at her gloves and takes them off.*) Oh dear, I am a mess. All covered with train soot. Do show me to the bathroom.

MAURICE. This way, auntie-tauntie. (MAURICE *goes up the right stairs.* ALICE *throws her gloves on the sofa on her way to the left stairs. But* MAURICE *has a necessary change of heart and comes tearing down the left stairs, frightening* ALICE *and stopping her in her tracks.*) No! Not this way!

ALICE. Now what's the matter?

MAURICE. Well, you see . . . (*Leading her towards the archway.*) It's this way. The best place to wash your hands is in the kitchen.

ALICE. The kitchen?!

MAURICE. Oh yes, it's lovely! Beautiful sink . . . lots of water . . . and, in the morning, the delicious aroma of coffee.

ALICE. But I'm not going to be washing all night.

MAURICE. Yes, it does something to me to smell coffee while I'm shaving at the sink.

ALICE. I may be behind the times but, I must say, I find these goings on astonishing. Are you sure no one's going to ask me to do the dishes?

MAURICE. Come, come, auntie-tauntie!

ALICE. Kindly refrain from calling me auntie-tauntie! I've ceased being your aunt until you see fit to marry! Think that one over, Maurice de Corneblanche. And now . . . to the kitchen! (*She goes out through the double doors.* MAURICE *dashes up the right stairs to the bedroom door.*)

MAURICE. (*Shouting.*) There's nobody here! You can come in now! (ALICE *returns.*)

ALICE. Maurice . . . (*A startled* MAURICE *comes sliding down the right stairs.*)

MAURICE. What?

ALICE. Who are you shouting to?

MAURICE. Shout? Oh, that. (*Going up the right stairs.*) It's the rule of the house. Every time one goes to the kitchen, one shouts: (*At the center of the platform, by the railing, facing the audience.*) 'There's nobody here! You can come in now!' (*He comes down the right stairs.*)

ALICE. What an incredible establishment! They've all lost their sense of direction.

MAURICE. I'll tell you the trouble. Their grandfather used to manufacture compasses. (*He leads* ALICE *towards the archway.*)

ALICE. I see no earthly connection between . . .

MAURICE. Poor souls, what a loss.

ALICE. Are you trying to tell me they lost their direction because they lost their compasses?

MAURICE. No. Their grandpapa. Poor dear dead grandpapa. (*They leave through the double doors.* HUGUETTE *comes in from the bedroom.*)

HUGUETTE. Well, I like that! . . . And now they're gone! (*Calling.*) Gaston! (*To herself, as she comes down the stairs.*) You can make yourself at home up to a point but this beats everything! (*Calling.*) Gaston! (GASTON, *smoothing his hair, comes in from the study.*)

GASTON. Yes, my love?

HUGUETTE. A moment ago I wished to come in here and his lordship . . . the vicomte . . . rushed to the door . . .

GASTON. To open it for you?

HUGUETTE. No, to keep it shut. He shouted, 'Don't come in! You can't come in! I'm locked in the arms of my beloved!'

GASTON. Clara?

HUGUETTE. Yes, Clara. Who else?

GASTON. (*Casting a startled glance towards the study.*) Clara. You don't say. That's curious.

HUGUETTE. I think he's taking too much for granted. Kissing and who knows what with that woman . . . in the middle of the afternoon . . . in my apartment . . . and keeping me shut out!

GASTON. But why did you want to come in, darling?

HUGUETTE. (*Not quite ready with her answer.*) Oh well, you see . . . I wanted to find out if you had stood firm on Didier.

GASTON. He's not leaving.

HUGUETTE. Not leaving?

GASTON. Actually he's gone up in my estimation.

HUGUETTE. Oh, you are contrary. If you'll push the divan into the boudoir, I'll put sheets on it for tonight. (*She goes up the stairs.*)

GASTON. Yes, I'll do it. I'll do it now. I'll do it right this minute. (HUGUETTE *goes into the boudoir.* GASTON *sits on the hassock.*) Kissing her and who knows what? But he couldn't have been. She was sitting on my knee! (*Struck by a sudden thought.*) Unless . . . My God! That's it! His old mistress . . . his real flame has turned up! She's here! Now what am I going to do? (*He turns around and there is* ALICE *coming back for her umbrella, which* DIDIER *had propped against the fireplace.*)

ALICE. Monsieur . . .

GASTON. Madame . . .

ALICE. Excuse me. I thought I'd left it in here. (*She looks behind the sofa for her umbrella.* GASTON *stares at her in astonishment.*) Where did he hide it? (*She looks on the left side of the French windows.*) It's not here . . . (*She looks on the right side of the French windows.*) It's not there . . .

GASTON. Hide what, madame?

ALICE. Napoleon.

GASTON. Napoleon?

ALICE. Yes. Napoleon Bonaparte. (*Spotting her Napoleon-headed umbrella.*) Ah, there he is! (*She picks up the umbrella.*) What an idiot!

GASTON. Who? Napoleon?

ALICE. No, your butler. The one who's wearing an overcoat and shivering.

GASTON. (*Now visibly upset.*) Oh, I see. The one who's wearing the overcoat and shivering . . .

ALICE. Oh, yes, before I forget . . . would you pass me my pair of handkerchiefs?

GASTON. Your pair of handkerchiefs?

ALICE. Yes, my brown suede pair of handkerchiefs. There . . . on the sofa.

GASTON. (*Holding up the gloves.*) These?

ALICE. Of course.

GASTON. Brown suede handkerchiefs?

ALICE. (*Taking the gloves.*) For a Parisian you're not very up-to-date, are you? It's the latest fashion, handkerchiefs with fingers. Obviously, you're not familiar with Louis Quatorze.

GASTON. What?

ALICE. He's been revived. (*She starts for the archway.*)

GASTON. (*To the audience, certain of her lunacy.*) Louis Quatorze . . . Napoleon!

ALICE. (*Turning back.*) Is this your apartment?

GASTON. Yes, madame.

ALICE. (*Going to him with a smile.*) Then . . . you're the compass-maker's grandson!

GASTON. (*More certain than ever of her insanity.*) The compass-maker?

ALICE. I do hope I didn't wake you up. It would disturb me to think I had.

GASTON. But I wasn't asleep.

ALICE. Now, now, no excuses! I hate the dark as much as you do at night!

GASTON. And in the daytime?

ALICE. Much less.

GASTON. I see, I see.

ALICE. Aren't you surprised I know so much about you?

GASTON. Well . . .

ALICE. It's not guesswork. They told me all about you when we were discussing the radiators.

GASTON. (*Humoring her.*) Oh, well, if they told you about the radiators, you were just passing by and dropped in to get warm.

ALICE. I did not. I came to see someone.

GASTON. And I know who it is . . . Maurice de Corneblanche!

ALICE. (*Giving him a sharp tap with her umbrella.*) That's him! Maurice de Corneblanche! The very mention of his name makes me furious! If you only knew how he's treated me! Let's not speak of it!

GASTON. No, let's not speak of it.

ALICE. No, let's do speak of it!

GASTON. All right.

ALICE. All right! Sit down! (GASTON *sits on the left chair.*) I'm taking my Maurice in hand! I won't let him run around loose any longer, exhausting himself in Paris and coming back to me as limp as a rag!

GASTON. Yes, you keep an eye on him!

ALICE. Leave it to me. His days of dissipation are over.

GASTON. Yes, I can see that.

ALICE. It's time he called a halt! . . . Would you do me a favor?

GASTON. If I can.

ALICE. Advise him to marry! You can well understand, at my age, one doesn't want to put off filling the nursery much longer.

GASTON. I'd say every second counts.

ALICE. There's nothing I wouldn't do to have those children!

GASTON. I'll take your word for it.

ALICE. Moreover, I have informed Maurice that if there's no marriage, there will be no more . . . anything. He'll get nothing whatever from me.

GASTON. (*Rises.*) Nothing?

ALICE. Nothing. My cupboard will be locked.

GASTON. What did he say?

ALICE. What could he say? I only hope by tonight he hasn't changed his mind. I like my Maurice best when he's . . . easy to manage. Well, au revoir, monsieur. (*She starts for the archway.*)

GASTON. (*Following her.*) Au revoir, madame!

ALICE. (*Turning back.*) And do forgive me for inflicting myself on you when you're in mourning.

GASTON. In mourning? Who's dead?

ALICE. Why, grandpapa! Poor dear grandpapa! (*She starts out, then returns.*) Oh! I almost forgot . . . (*She quickly goes up the right stairs, stands outside the boudoir door, by the railing, facing the audience, and shouts:*) There's nobody here! You can come in now! (*Very pleased with this little effort, she comes down the stairs and goes up to* GASTON *again. He is more alarmed than ever.*) That's because I'm going to the kitchen.

GASTON. The kitchen?

ALICE. Yes, to powder my nose and smell the coffee. (*She leaves through the double doors.*)

GASTON. To powder her nose and smell the coffee. Well, I hope it's perking! Grandpapa! (*He rises.*) Whose grandpapa? My God, I am sorry for Corneblanche. How she must have changed since he last saw her! (*He shrugs.*) Oh! Well! (*Looking towards the study.*) Clara! Where's my Clara! (*In full fervor and with fancy footwork,* GASTON *enters the study, but immediately* HUGUETTE *comes in from the boudoir.*)

HUGUETTE. Gaston! I thought you were moving the divan into my boudoir. (GASTON *shifts into reverse, comes out of the study and goes up the stairs.*)

GASTON. Yes, yes, I was just going to . . . as you can see, I'm on my way. (*He goes into the boudoir.* ROSINE *comes in from the bedroom.*)

HUGUETTE. I'm free now, if you'd like to go out somewhere.

ROSINE. (*Who has changed her dress.*) No, thanks. I have an escort. (*She comes down the stairs.*)

HUGUETTE. What?

ROSINE. I found what I'm looking for.

HUGUETTE. A man?

ROSINE. Of course, a man.

HUGUETTE. Where did you find him?

ROSINE. Here in your apartment. He's very charming.

HUGUETTE. Good heavens! Not the hero of the love story I've been telling you about!

ROSINE. Oh, no! Is he the one?

HUGUETTE. And he's already taken. Rosine, why don't you talk things over with your fiance?

ROSINE. Him! I should go running after him! Why,

I wouldn't marry Maurice de Corneblanche if he was . . .

HUGUETTE. What? What name did you say?

ROSINE. Maurice de Corneblanche.

HUGUETTE. Oh, dear. (*Grasping the whole situation.*) What have I done?

ROSINE. Done?

HUGUETTE. I've been encouraging him to resume his affair with his former mistress!

ROSINE. What of it?

HUGUETTE. But, Rosine, it's . . . *him!*

ROSINE. Him?

HUGUETTE. The previous tenant of this apartment . . . and the man you're refusing to marry . . . are one and the same! (*She rushes into the bedroom.*)

ROSINE. What? Oh, no! (*To the audience, furiously.*) The man I planned to use to make a fool of Maurice . . . is Maurice himself! Oh!!! (DIDIER, *still wearing the overcoat, comes in through the double doors.*)

DIDIER. (*Relieved.*) Phew! She's gone!

ROSINE. (*Turning on him.*) There you are!

DIDIER. Yes!

ROSINE. And I see you're ready to go out!

DIDIER. Ready? Oh, yes. (*Buttoning the last button.*) I . . . I have my coat on. See? Well, let's be on our way.

ROSINE. Let's not! I've changed my mind!

DIDIER. Why?

ROSINE. I detest you!

DIDIER. But . . . what have I done?

ROSINE. I've discovered you're Maurice de Corneblanche. Well, I'm Rosine Rose. The girl you were supposed to marry!

DIDIER. No! What fun! Delighted to meet you!

Rosine. A delight you could have enjoyed long ago!

Didier. And would, if I had known.

Rosine. (*Hurling it at him.*) I was in love with you! Yes! Without even knowing you! I idolized you! You were my dream lover! And now you have the nerve to look exactly like what I thought you'd look like! . . . Well, I know what I'm going to do!

Didier. What?

Rosine. Take a lover! You have a mistress, I'll take a lover!

Didier. I forbid it!

Rosine. Would that bother you?

Didier. Perhaps it would.

Rosine. Perhaps? (*She sits on the sofa.*)

Didier. What a delightful child you are.

Rosine. I am not a child!

Didier. No, you're not. You're a darling. (*He sits beside her.*)

Rosine. Am I, Maurice?

Didier. Yes, Rosine . . . dear, little Rosine. (Maurice *appears at the French windows.*)

Rosine. (*Hopefully.*) Then you're not just an overnight boy looking for another overnight girl?

Didier. You have the wrong opinion of me, Rosine. I want a girl who's good for a thousand and one nights.

Rosine. A thousand and one? That's not very many. I wouldn't even be twenty-three.

Didier. My silly white goose, at twenty you can love on and on to a thousand, thousand and one nights. (Maurice *has crept behind the sofa, unseen by* Didier *and* Rosine.)

Rosine. (*Ready to let herself be convinced.*) Then you're sorry?

Didier. Very sorry.

Rosine. How very?

Didier. Very, very. (*From behind the sofa,* Maurice *thumps* Didier *on the head.* Didier, *staggered, rises.*) I mean . . .

Rosine. What?

Didier. I . . . I . . . (*From behind the sofa,* Maurice *threatens him.*) I'd be very sorry to have to give up my collection of overnight girls for one simple, inexperienced Pollyanna from the provinces!

Rosine. Oh, you! How could you! (*She rises.*)

Didier. Why didn't you enquire first? Anyone could have told you that Maurice de Corneblanche is a worthless rake who lives on his wits, sponges on his friends, spends his days at the races and his nights in the Place Pigalle! (Maurice *pops up from behind the sofa, looking displeased, then pops down again. Throughout, he remains unseen by* Rosine.)

Rosine. Oh, you . . . you . . . you! You are a monster!

Didier. Yes, a monster! Take my advice, forget him! (*Directly to* Maurice *behind the sofa.*) He's pig swill! (Maurice *rises and picks up the vase of roses from the pedestal, which he would like to throw at* Didier.)

Rosine. How you revel in your shame! I'm sorry I ever met you, Maurice de Corneblanche! (*She runs into the bedroom.*)

Didier. Well, how did I do? She won't make the mistake of falling in love with me. I blackened your name good.

Maurice. Personally, I think you went too far on my behalf.

Didier. Imagine reaching twenty without belonging to a man! (*He sits on the octagonal table.*)

Maurice. Just see she never belongs to you!

DIDIER. She won't. Not now. She's going to cheat on me.

MAURICE. On you? On me! I'm the one she's going to cheat on. (*Proudly.*) Me! Me! (*Suddenly realizes what he's saying.*) Oh, my God! (*He leaves through the double doors.* HUGUETTE *comes in from the bedroom.*)

HUGUETTE. Monsieur, I must speak to you on a very delicate matter.

DIDIER. Yes?

HUGUETTE. I want to help you to see the dangers in picking up the threads of a past romance.

DIDIER. You're against it?

HUGUETTE. Yes, I am!

DIDIER. (*Delighted.*) Really?

HUGUETTE. Clara is very nice. But are her moral standards as high as when you used to know her?

DIDIER. Well, time changes everyone.

HUGUETTE. Indeed it does. And once love has been exhausted, disillusionment prevails.

DIDIER. Yes, it's sad.

HUGUETTE. Very sad. (*Looking at the bedroom, where* ROSINE *is.*) But a new love, fresh and rich with promise . . . isn't that preferable to the hope of reviving a handful of ashes?

DIDIER. (*Who has not caught her look, misunderstands and believes* HUGUETTE *is offering herself.*) Oh, indeed it is!

HUGUETTE. So you won't be spending the night here.

DIDIER. What? After what you've just said? Nothing can stop me!

HUGUETTE. (*To the audience.*) He hasn't understood a word . . . (GASTON *comes in from the boudoir.*)

GASTON. Huguette, I moved the divan into the

boudoir. It's very comfortable. I'll sleep in there if you like.

HUGUETTE. Alone?

GASTON. Of course, alone. You'd better stay in our room with Rosine.

HUGUETTE. Yes. She's terribly upset.

GASTON. Then stay with her all night! Don't leave her for a second! It's important, vitally important! Poor little thing.

HUGUETTE. Yes, she's our responsibility. We shouldn't take any chances. (*She goes into the bedroom.*)

GASTON. (*Calling after* HUGUETTE.) That's right, dear. We shouldn't take any chances! (*He races down the left stairs to sit beside* DIDIER.) Now quick. Here's the plan for tonight. Are you listening?

DIDIER. Yes.

GASTON. You'll sleep in here.

DIDIER. With Clara?

GASTON. (*With authority.*) Yes!

DIDIER. (*Spontaneously.*) Good!

GASTON. In principle only, that is.

DIDIER. (*Deflated.*) Oh.

GASTON. As soon as everybody's asleep, I'll come in here and take your place. Understand?

DIDIER. Perfectly. Then what happens.

GASTON. (*Rises.*) You'll stretch out in my study . . . on a soft, springy sofa just right for you and your lady love.

DIDIER. Clara? (*He rises.*) You're going to send Clara in to me?

GASTON. Funny fellow! No, not Clara . . . the *other* one . . . the really *old* flame.

DIDIER. (*Confused.*) The really . . . ?

GASTON. Yes! She's showed up! I saw her only a while ago!

DIDIER. You don't say.

GASTON. She'll be back later tonight.

DIDIER. (*Stupefied.*) You've actually been talking to her?

GASTON. What a conversation! But tell me, have you seen her recently or simply spoken to her over the phone?

DIDIER. (*Who doesn't know what to answer.*) Um . . . on the phone. It's all been done on the phone.

GASTON. I was afraid of that! You must be brave. (*He pats* DIDIER *on the shoulder.*) You'll have to be!

DIDIER. Brave? Why?

GASTON. Because she is changed. Very, very much changed.

DIDIER. She is?

GASTON. How you must have made her suffer! . . . It's true, I never knew her before but if she hasn't changed, then I've never encountered such chivalry in all my life! (MAURICE *comes in from the hall.*)

MAURICE. Monsieur, the new bedroom furniture has arrived.

GASTON. Thank you. (*To* DIDIER.) I'll tell Clara what we've arranged. Oh, by the way, she also said she's keeping her cupboard locked, *unless . . . !*

DIDIER. Clara said that?

GASTON. No, not Clara. The other one. Old Mother Hubbard.

DIDIER. Unless what?

GASTON. Unless you give her a legitimate child! (*He goes into the study.*)

DIDIER. (*To* MAURICE.) Where's this all going to end? Now I have a third woman to juggle with the other two!

MAURICE. Who is she?

DIDIER. I don't know! Some old mistress or something. You heard him. And, what's more, this one wants to put *me* in the family way! (*He goes out down the hall,* MAURICE *following.* CLARA *rushes out of the study towards the French windows,* GASTON *following.*)

CLARA. Not now, Gaston! Not now!

GASTON. Why not now?

CLARA. Because I want to see the furniture!

GASTON. Can't you wait?

CLARA. If you can't wait, why should I?

GASTON. Wait, at least, until they get the furniture out of the van!

CLARA. (*Looking out the French windows.*) Oh! Look at the color! It's cyclamen!

GASTON. Careful! Careful, my man! Leave the pouffe there and bring in the bed! (*To* CLARA.) The bed! Love's final destination!

CLARA. Oh Gaston, Gaston, it's madness! What will you think of me?

GASTON. I'll tell you later! (MAURICE *comes in from the hall, unseen by* CLARA *and* GASTON.)

CLARA. Oh, yes! . . . Oh, no! (*She pretends to fend him off but really hugs him.*) Oh, my darling! Oh, my dearest! Oh, I don't want to!

GASTON. Oh, I know you don't!

CLARA. Oh, don't say that!

GASTON. Oh! (*He almost kisses her.*)

MAURICE. (*To* CLARA.) Belt! (GASTON *and* CLARA *fly apart.*)

GASTON. (*To* MAURICE.) What did you say?

MAURICE. Belt! The living belt!

GASTON. (*Furiously.*) What do you mean by interfering?

MAURICE. But monsieur told me not to leave this lady alone with anybody.

GASTON. You fool! That didn't include me!

CLARA. (*To* MAURICE.) You did right to interfere. Keep it up. For my sake. I must have a man who's free or no man at all. (*To* GASTON.) Besides your wife's so charming! (DIDIER *comes in from the hall.*)

GASTON. (*To* MAURICE.) I'd like to wring your neck! Now start taking this furniture out of here!

MAURICE. Who? Me?

GASTON. Who else?

MAURICE. Oh no, I couldn't.

DIDIER. (*Butting in.*) Do as you're told! You present a very bad picture to a guest.

MAURICE. (*Bent on revenge.*) And how do you think you look to a servant? Losing your shirt tail in mixed company!

DIDIER. What?

MAURICE. (*Pointing to the apron showing below* DIDIER's *overcoat.*) There! It's hanging out! Down there! (CLARA *sits on the octagonal table for a closer look.*)

CLARA. Oh!

GASTON. Well, so it is!

DIDIER. (*Mortified.*) I wonder what it's doing out?

MAURICE. I wonder.

GASTON. So do I. (DIDIER *slips his hand inside the coat and starts to pull up the apron.*)

CLARA. Oh, look! It's disappearing! (CLARA, GASTON *and* MAURICE *laugh.* DIDIER *is all at sea.*)

GASTON. (*To* CLARA.) This is no fit sight for you, my dear. (*To* DIDIER.) Adjust yourself, monsieur! Adjust yourself!

CURTAIN

ACT THREE

Scene: *While the set is the same, the furnishings have been changed. At far right center in front of the fireplace is a small chaise. A large bed with a silk-quilted headboard has replaced the chair and cabinet. An extra large circular pouffe with a centerpiece has replaced the sofa. Upstage left of the pouffe and below the platform is a delicate dressing table and chair. At left and right of the bed are small bedside tables. A bed lamp adorns the headboard. An easy to carry three-section folding screen of medium height, covered in the same material as the headboard and coverlet, has been placed left of the right bedside table. The large rubber plant on the stand is next to the screen. New draperies surround the bed unit.*

Time: *After dinner.*

As the curtain rises, Maurice, *with a log carrier, comes in from the hall and goes to the fireplace.*

Maurice. (*Grumbling.*) Waiting on table! Poking the fire! I do all the work . . . Didier all the women! (*He puts down the log carrier.* Rosine, *upset, comes in from the hall, followed by* Huguette, *who switches on the main light.* Huguette *is wearing an evening dress.* Rosine *wears the same dress as in the preceding act.*)

Rosine. Forgive me, Huguette, for jumping up from dinner.

Huguette. It's all right, Rosine. I understand.

Rosine. It was quite obvious Maurice and that Clara are going to be inseparable until morning. It wasn't necessary for Gaston to repeat it with each course.

Huguette. Yes, Gaston is behaving in a most peculiar way.

Rosine. Huguette, do you mind if I go into the bedroom?

Huguette. Do, dear. I'll join you in a few moments. (Rosine *goes up the stairs.*) Rosine! Why don't you forget him once and for all?

Rosine. I can't. Not yet. Huguette, I brought a negligee with me. A naughty one!

Huguette. A naughty one? Rosine, what's come over you?

Rosine. I'm going to show this Maurice de Corneblanche what really blooms in the country! (*She goes into the bedroom.*)

Huguette. But she's only a bud . . . and the first strong breeze . . .

Maurice. Exactly! We don't want any blossoms in the dust! Do we, madame?

Huguette. No, we don't. Oh, it's you again, Didier! (Clara *comes in from the hall, followed by* Didier *and* Gaston. Clara *is in an evening dress, the men are in dinner jackets.*)

Clara. (*Admiring the room.*) Why it's adorable!

Didier. Do you really like it?

Clara. It's heavenly! (*To* Huguette.) Don't you agree?

HUGUETTE. Yes. It simply cries out for someone to spend the night in it. (DIDIER *swings around and looks lovingly at* HUGUETTE, *while* GASTON *swings around to* CLARA.)

GASTON & DIDIER. How very true!

DIDIER. (*Looking at* HUGUETTE.) Especially with the one you adore.

GASTON. Yes, you lucky dog! How I'd like to be in your pajamas!

HUGUETTE. Gaston!

GASTON. Oh. I meant . . . only if you were there, darling. (*To* MAURICE, *at the fireplace*.) Don't you have any idea how to kindle a flame? Give it air . . . freedom . . .

CLARA. (*Going towards the fireplace*.) Let me do it. I know how to revive a slumbering fire. Use a blow-pipe. (*She sits on the chaise and crosses her legs*.) Shall I show you, Gaston?

GASTON. Well . . . (*He catches a suspicious look from* HUGUETTE.) Not right this minute, Clara! (*He quickly picks up the log carrier, thrusts it into* MAURICE's *hands and rushes him out of the room*.)

DIDIER. (*To* CLARA.) You shouldn't give away all our secrets, darling. (*To* HUGUETTE.) Won't you sit down, madame?

GASTON. (*With spirit, as he stops* HUGUETTE *from sitting*.) Sit down? Are you sure you want to, Huguette? (*Looking at* CLARA *and* DIDIER.) It hardly seems fair to keep prolonging the evening. Not that I'm rushing everyone to bed.

HUGUETTE. Yes, Gaston. You're right. (*She goes up the stairs. To* DIDIER.) If you find you still need anything, don't hesitate to call.

DIDIER. Indeed I shall.

GASTON. (*Going up the stairs to* HUGUETTE.) Need? What could they possibly need, dear, except to be left alone? Now off you go to Rosine. We must leave the lovers to their own devices. (*He pushes* HUGUETTE *into the bedroom and calls after her:*) Sleep like a log, dear! (*He quickly closes the door and rushes down the right stairs.*) Alone at last! (*He pushes* DIDIER *on to the bed as he passes him.*) Excuse me.

CLARA. Not so fast, Gaston! Be sweet! Be kind! Be gentle!

GASTON. (*Sitting next to her.*) Why should I? Everything's permitted now.

DIDIER. Excuse me, monsieur. Do you want me to watch the whole night?

GASTON. I should say not! (*He rises.*) But for safety's sake, stay until I make certain. I'll go in the boudoir and slam a few drawers. (*He goes up the stairs.*) Once Huguette hears me in there she'll relax. (*To* CLARA.) Then I'll slip out quietly and back into your arms! (GASTON *goes into the boudoir, blowing kisses to* CLARA *until he disappears.*)

CLARA. (*To* DIDIER.) I feel strange . . . the two of us . . . alone . . . with a bed.

DIDIER. I know what you mean.

CLARA. If you play with matches . . .

DIDIER. Yes, you set off the fireworks.

CLARA. But it's funny, isn't it, that now with nobody around we don't dare let even our fingertips touch. (*She sits on the pouffe.*)

DIDIER. No, we don't, do we? (*He leans on the centerpiece of the pouffe.*)

CLARA. I wonder what our lovely love-life of long ago was really like.

DIDIER. Well, we can't take a trip back into the past, can we? (*He sits on the pouffe.*)

CLARA. No, we can't. We must push forward. (*She slides on the pouffe, getting close to him.*) That's not too close, is it?

DIDIER. No, I think we should push on. (*He inches closer to her.*)

CLARA. It's not too close for comfort?

DIDIER. Not yet! (*He takes her in his arms.*)

CLARA. (*Holding him tight.*) Oh, please, monsieur, don't push your luck too far! (MAURICE *comes in from the hall.*)

MAURICE. Watch out there! (CLARA *and* DIDIER *jump up.*)

CLARA. What?

MAURICE. Cool off! Unless you want him to snap the belt, madame!

CLARA. The belt?

MAURICE. He's stretching it!

CLARA. Saved again. Thank you, monsieur.

MAURICE. The living belt . . . at your service! (*He goes into the study.*)

CLARA. He came in the nick of time.

DIDIER. Only just.

CLARA. You must do me a favor.

DIDIER. Whatever you say.

CLARA. Change places with me. *You* sleep with Gaston.

DIDIER. Me? You want me to sleep with him?

CLARA. Yes. Do it for me. Please, monsieur.

DIDIER. In my state, you're asking me to sleep with Woody Boy? (GASTON *re-enters from the boudoir and comes down the stairs.*)

GASTON. Well, that should do it. Huguette can go to

sleep with a contented mind. (*To* CLARA.) And so can we. (*To* DIDIER.) Monsieur de Corneblanche, the study is through there. (DIDIER *goes to the study.*)

CLARA. (*Uneasily to* DIDIER.) You're not going, are you?

DIDIER. Yes, the time has come.

GASTON. On your way out, switch off the light. (DIDIER *does so.*) Oh, Clara darling, don't you love this intimate glow! . . . See you in the morning, monsieur. (*There is a knock on the bedroom door.*) Wait! Somebody's at the door!

CLARA. (*Delighted at the intrusion.*) Come in! Come in! (*Aside.*) Thank God, whoever you are! (GASTON *rushes to escape in the direction of the archway.* HUGUETTE *comes in from the bedroom.*)

GASTON. My wife! (*He picks up the large rubber plant from the stand, then sits on the stand, holding the rubber plant in front of his face.* DIDIER, *about to leave, quickly shuts the study door and comes back into the room.*)

HUGUETTE. (*To* DIDIER.) Excuse me . . . were you after something?

DIDIER. Er . . . no . . . yes! . . . that is, a glass of water.

HUGUETTE. See, I was sure you might need something. (*As she comes down the stairs and goes towards the bedside table, she spots* GASTON.) Gaston, what are you doing there?

GASTON. (*Peering out from behind the rubber plant.*) Who? Me? (*He rises.*) I . . . I also came in to get him a glass of water.

HUGUETTE. I'll take care of it. You go to bed.

GASTON. Yes, yes, I'm going. But don't leave Rosine alone too long! (*He goes up the stairs. To* CLARA *and*

DIDIER.) Good night. See you in the morning. Good night.

CLARA. Good night!

GASTON. (*Throwing kisses to* CLARA *from behind the rubber plant.*) Good night!

DIDIER. (*Sharply.*) Good night!

HUGUETTE. Good night!

GASTON. Good night. (*He goes into the boudoir with the rubber plant.*)

HUGUETTE. I'll get the water. (*She picks up the carafe on the bedside table.*) Oh, you already have some . . .

DIDIER. Oh, so we do, don't we?

HUGUETTE. So I suppose there's nothing left for me to do but to leave.

CLARA. (*With spirit.*) No, stay!

DIDIER. Yes, do stay! We'd love to have you.

HUGUETTE. Oh, I see what's the matter! (*She sits at the foot of the bed.*) You have the jitters. Well, I feel a bit . . . quakey myself. This brings back memories of my wedding night. (*She rises.*) Oh, no! You wouldn't want *me* to sleep here.

DIDIER. Oh, yes we would. (*He has her sit on the bed again, then sits beside her.*)

CLARA. If it's not asking too much, dear Huguette. (*She sits on the other side of* HUGUETTE.)

HUGUETTE. The three of us? Together?

CLARA. Of course not. I'll sleep in the study.

HUGUETTE. In the study? Now I know you're making fun of me. (*She heaves a sigh. A pause. She turns and looks into* DIDIER's *eyes, then turns to* CLARA.) Good night. (*It looks as though she's asking* CLARA *to leave, but* CLARA *doesn't budge.*)

CLARA. Good night.

HUGUETTE. (*To* DIDIER.) Good night. (*She rises and goes up the stairs.*)

DIDIER. Good night. (*He rises and follows her to the foot of the stairs.*)

HUGUETTE. (*Sighs.*) Good night. (*She goes into the bedroom.*)

DIDIER. I wonder how long we've got before someone else comes in?

CLARA. I wonder.

DIDIER. Now where were we?

CLARA. Where we shouldn't be. . . . Well? Why not? (*She falls back on the bed, throwing her arms wide open.* DIDIER *bends over to kiss her.* MAURICE *comes in from the hall.*)

MAURICE. (*Switching on the main light.*) *Belt!* (CLARA *and* DIDIER *fly apart.*)

DIDIER. Oh! (*He rises.*) Again!

CLARA. Thank you! (*She rises.*)

DIDIER. Are you going to be prowling around like this all night?

MAURICE. Yes, monsieur. On the same tracks, like a railroad train.

DIDIER. What railroad train?

MAURICE. (*Doing a "choo-choo" train shuffle around the chaise.*) The one that goes round and round. It is known as The Southern (*To* CLARA.) *Belt* Line! (*He makes the sound of a train whistle.*) And may I remind monsieur someone is going to come ringing at the front door . . . and it's up to monsieur to answer it! Toot! Toot! (*He choo-choo train shuffles down the hall.*)

DIDIER. (*Following him up to the archway. Furiously.*) Toot! Toot!

CLARA. (*Calling him back.*) Toot! Toot! (*Meaning 'remember me?'*)

DIDIER. Toot! Toot! (*Meaning 'will you?'*)

CLARA. (*Lovingly.*) Toot! Toot! (*Meaning 'yes.'* *She sits on the bed.*)

DIDIER. (*Enraptured.*) Toot! Toot! (*Meaning 'I have it made.' He sits beside her on the bed.*) Oh, you lovely creature! (*They are about to embrace again, when* GASTON'S *head pops in through the boudoir door.*)

GASTON. Has my wife gone?

DIDIER. Yes, you can come in.

GASTON. (*Coming down the stairs.*) Well, see you in the morning for coffee!

DIDIER. (*Rises.*) Yes, monsieur. I'm sure we'll all need a cup by then. (*He heads for the study.*)

GASTON. Oh, one more thing. This old flame of yours . . . when she gets back, see that she doesn't meet my wife.

DIDIER. Yes . . . of course. (*As he leaves.*) But who the devil is she? (*He goes into the study.*)

GASTON. Clara, this is it! Alone at last!

CLARA. Oh, Gaston! I want to give myself to you. And I'm going to . . . but on one condition: Will you do the same as me?

GASTON. But won't we both be doing the same thing at the same time?

CLARA. I mean get a divorce.

GASTON. Wait until I'm divorced! But Clara, that's like asking Mount Vesuvius in eruption to hold everything until leap year! (*He sits on the chaise.*)

CLARA. Oh, Gaston! (*She sits beside him.*)

GASTON. Oh, Clara! (*He takes her in his arms.* MAURICE *comes in from the hall.*)

MAURICE. (*Very softly.*) Good night, monsieur. (CLARA *and* GASTON *leap up.*)

GASTON. What are you doing back?

MAURCE. I remembered I hadn't said good night to monsieur. I couldn't sleep unless I had. Good night, monsieur.

GASTON. (*Dryly.*) Good night.

MAURICE. (*With a charming smile.*) Good night.

GASTON. (*Furiously.*) Good night! Don't think I'm not touched but tonight I don't need your affection!

MAURICE. (*To* CLARA.) *Belt!* (*He shuffles up to the archway.*) Toot! Toot! (*And goes out down the hall.*)

GASTON. (*Enraged, following* MAURICE *up the archway.*) Toot! Toot! The crazy fool!

CLARA. (*Stopping him.*) No, Gaston. (GASTON *stops, turns, looks admiringly at* CLARA *and melts. He switches off the main light.*)

GASTON. Oh, Clara! (*Slowly he starts to pursue her.*)

CLARA. Gaston, no! Gaston! Oh, Gaston!

GASTON. There's no turning back!

CLARA. At least give me time to undress.

GASTON. I've nothing against that!

CLARA. Set up the screen for me.

GASTON. The screen?

CLARA. Over there. Set it up here for me.

GASTON. (*Disappointed, his face dropping.*) If that's what you want. (*While* GASTON *fetches the screen,* CLARA *takes a nightgown from her suitcase and puts it on the pouffe.* GASTON *sets up the screen but craftily opens only one panel. He sits on the bed and is able to watch* CLARA *undress with an unhampered view. So can the audience.*) Mother Nature was more than generous to you.

CLARA. She certainly was. (CLARA *catches* GASTON *looking at her. She jumps, surprised, then draws out the screen to its full length, not across the room but towards the audience, blocking* GASTON'S *view. Throughout the following,* GASTON *and* CLARA *play hide-and-seek around the screen.* GASTON *periodically jumps up, trying to look over the screen. He is not too successful so he stands on the bed and bounces there.*) Oh, naughty Gaston! . . . Naughty! . . . Play fair! . . . Don't come near me! . . . Don't peek!

GASTON. But I want to look at you first just as you are.

CLARA. Stay on your side! . . . Please! . . . Be nice. Pass me my nightie! . . . Come on, Gaston, throw it over to me! (GASTON *takes the nightgown from the pouffe. With his back to the audience, he deliberately tosses the nightgown on to the bed. Then he takes up a runner's position, downstage left, ready to race over and trap* CLARA *on the bed the moment she goes for the nightgown.* CLARA, *on the other side of the screen, sizes up the situation and holds her runner's position downstage right. Then, she races to the bed and grabs her nightgown, beating* GASTON *to it. He goes sprawling on the bed. She rushes over to the chaise, where she puts on her nightgown.*) Keep your distance! Let's prolong this ecstasy. Go away and come back in fifteen minutes!

GASTON. Fifteen minutes?!

CLARA. Yes. You can't refuse me such a tiny request. I want to play the 'Good Girl' game.

GASTON. The 'Good Girl' game? What's that?

CLARA. I'll get into bed alone. I'll put out the light. I'll pretend I'm asleep . . . like a good girl. Then you'll come in and surprise me in the dark!

GASTON. Well, that's one way of doing it. (*Looking at his watch.*) Fifteen minutes. Thank God my watch is running fast! (*There is a knock on the bedroom door.*) Somebody's at the door!

CLARA. Come in! (HUGUETTE *comes in from the bedroom and comes down the stairs.* GASTON *quickly folds the screen and puts it back against the wall.*)

GASTON. Caught again! (*He sits on the stand, which formerly held the rubber plant, and covers his face with both his hands.*)

HUGUETTE. (*Spotting him.*) Gaston! Are you still here?

GASTON. (*Taking his hands from his face.*) Oh, no!

HUGUETTE. What do you mean, 'oh, no'?

GASTON. I mean I left my cigarettes behind. I came back to get them. But what about you, Darling?

HUGUETTE. I left my lighter behind.

GASTON. How extraordinary.

HUGUETTE. Do you mind if I look around, Clara?

CLARA. Oh, do. Please do. (HUGUETTE *goes to the dressing table, then to the bedside table near the French windows.*)

GASTON. (*To* CLARA, *as he goes up the right stairs.*) You will pardon the intrusion, madame. I shan't disturb you again. (*He turns to* HUGUETTE.) Excuse me, darling. (*He blows kisses to* CLARA, *behind* HUGUETTE'S *back.* HUGUETTE *turns and almost catches him.*) Excuse me! (*He goes into the boudoir.*)

HUGUETTE. How odd, I can't find it.

CLARA. Perhaps you left it in the study! I'll go and look for it.

HUGUETTE. Don't bother! It doesn't matter!

CLARA. No bother at all! You're doing me a favor! (*She goes quickly into the study.*)

HUGUETTE. (*To the audience.*) How strange! Rosine will keep sending me in here but somehow I don't seem to mind. What's come over me? (DIDIER *comes in from the study and switches on the light.*) You.

DIDIER. I understand you need a light, madame.

HUGUETTE. Yes. But I can use a match. (*She starts to leave.*)

DIDIER. Don't go! I've been thinking over what you told me before dinner.

HUGUETTE. About what?

DIDIER. Picking up the threads of my past romance with Clara. I agree, it would be foolish to try. But I need your help.

HUGUETTE. How?

DIDIER. To create a rift between Clara and me.

HUGUETTE. A rift?

DIDIER. Something that will keep us apart forever.

HUGUETTE. Well, there's nothing I can do.

DIDIER. Oh, yes, there is.

HUGUETTE. What?

DIDIER. Your husband isn't joining you tonight so come and spend the night here with me.

HUGUETTE. Spend the night with you?

DIDIER. Yes. We can talk.

HUGUETTE. Talk? All night?

DIDIER. I can keep it up.

HUGUETTE. But your Clara will think all sorts of things.

DIDIER. Exactly. That's what we want her to think.

HUGUETTE. You're asking too much of me. No, it's impossible.

DIDIER. That's too bad. It's too bad for Clara . . . and it's too bad for Rosine.

HUGUETTE. Rosine?

DIDIER. Yes, she and Clara could both be cured of me in one night with you, madame!

HUGUETTE. No! You're placing too heavy a responsibility on me.

DIDIER. You know best. We'll drop the subject.

HUGUETTE. But if I did do such a foolish thing, would you behave with the strictest propriety?

DIDIER. Oh! Absolutely! You know me.

HUGUETTE. Not all that well yet.

DIDIER. Then this will be your opportunity.

HUGUETTE. But if my husband finds out . . . No!

DIDIER. (*Coming close to her.*) I'll never tell him. My word of honor.

HUGUETTE. Well, if I do do it, it will be only for Rosine.

DIDIER. That's it. Do it for her.

HUGUETTE. Well . . .

DIDIER. For her!

HUGUETTE. Well, only for her. But it's madness! (*He takes her in his arms. The front doorbell rings. MAURICE bursts in through the double doors.*)

MAURICE. That's it! That's it! The doorbell's ringing!

HUGUETTE. (*Coming out of DIDIER's embrace. To MAURICE, in a fury of frustration.*) Well, answer it! (*She rises from the pouffe.*) You don't have to warn the whole house every time the doorbell rings! (*She goes up the stairs and into the bedroom. The doorbell rings again.*)

MAURICE. (*To DIDIER.*) It's Aunt Alice! I know it is! Here, get into this! (*He gives DIDIER his white coat. DIDIER quickly gets out of his dinner jacket so he can swap with MAURICE.*)

DIDIER. She'll spoil everything! And just when I had Huguette in the mood!

MAURICE. (*In the dinner jacket.*) Hurry up before she rings again!

DIDIER. (*In the white servant's coat.*) And you, for heaven's sake, try and look natural! (*He shoves MAU-RICE on to the chaise and puts him in a comic "nat-ural" position by crossing MAURICE's legs and holding out one of his hands.*) There! Relax! (*The doorbell rings again.*) All right, all right! We know you're there! (*He rushes out through the double doors.*)

MAURICE. If anybody comes in now, I've had it! (*He hears someone at the study door.*) Oh, here's someone already! What shall I do? (*In panic, he rises, darts forward, then back to the chaise. He kneels on the chaise and buries his head so no one can see his face. His rump is in the air.* CLARA *enters from the study.*)

CLARA. It's no good! I can't fight it any longer! (*She makes a complete circle around the chaise, from left to right, stopping at the foot of the chaise right. Mistaking* MAURICE *for* DIDIER, *she kneels and slaps* MAURICE *on the rump with both her hands, while looking out front to the audience.*) Don't look at me, Monsieur de Corneblanche! Don't look at me!

MAURICE. (*With his head still buried, he turns and looks out so only the audience can see his face.*) Don't worry. I won't.

CLARA. (*Rising and going back around the chaise to its left side.*) I'm so ashamed. But I can't help it. I've come to give myself to you!

MAURICE. (*Doing the same business as above.*) You have!

CLARA. That fool of a butler has left me unpro-tected! (*Opening wide her arms.*) Take me! I'm yours!

MAURICE. (*Standing up on the chaise, revealing himself to* CLARA.) *Belt!*

CLARA. Oh? You! The belt of Providence! (*Indicating his dinner jacket.*) But what are you doing dressed like that?

MAURICE. (*With authority.*) It's none of your business! (*Pointing to the study.*) Get back in there!

CLARA. (*Indignantly.*) You fool! Aren't you forgetting your station?

MAURICE. (*Stepping off the chaise.*) I am not a fool and I am not a butler! I am Didier! *Didier Larue!*

CLARA. Who did you say?

MAURICE. Didier Larue, the novelist. I am enduring this masquerade to acquire material for my new book.

CLARA. No! . . . Didier Larue! . . . I've read you . . . and loved you right through to the end! Oh! It's unbelievable! (*She runs into his arms.*)

MAURICE. Yes, isn't it?

CLARA. Won't Gaston be surprised!

MAURICE. No! Not a word to anybody! In return for your sealed lips, I'll continue my tight watch over you.

CLARA. (*Profile to profile with* MAURICE, *she turns her face to the audience.*) It takes a tough hide to be a butler.

MAURICE. (*Turning his face to the audience.*) It takes a tougher hide to be a belt.

CLARA. Don't leave me alone. I'll be waiting for you . . . (*She starts towards the study, then turns back.*) Didier Larue! Oh, it's too thrilling! (*She starts again for the study.*) Come quickly! Come quickly!

MAURICE. What for?

CLARA. (*Turning and rushing back into the room.*) I have a novel opening for your new book! (*Elated, she goes into the study, closing the door behind her.)*

MAURICE. Why didn't I say Didier Larue before? Who knows how many more fans he has? (*He starts for the study but is deflected as* DIDIER *comes in through the double doors. He is now wearing the apron underneath the white coat. He is arguing with* ALICE, *who is as determined to come in as* DIDIER *is to keep her out. She is trying to get in from the outside, turning the handle of the door, to which* DIDIER *is clinging from the inside.)* The catastrophe!

DIDIER. No! No! You can't come in!

MAURICE. It's all right. I'm alone!

DIDIER. (*Shouting.*) It's all right! You can come in! (*He opens the door and politely makes way for* ALICE *to enter.*) Would mademoiselle care to enter? (*An outraged* ALICE *comes in.*)

ALICE. Maurice, I can guarantee this butler won't remain in this house much longer!

DIDIER. (*Indicating* MAURICE.) I thought monsieur was undressing . . . in fact, naked. I was trying to spare mademoiselle a painful sight.

ALICE. (*Indignantly.*) Painful? Let me tell you not since Great-uncle Louis has any Corneblanche had reason to be ashamed of his anatomy!

MAURICE. (*Striking a muscle man pose.*) That's true!

ALICE. (*Looking around.*) But isn't there something different about this room?

MAURICE. Oh, just a little bit.

DIDIER. Yes, just a little bit.

ALICE. You've changed it!

MAURICE. I can't hide a thing from you, auntie, can I?

ALICE. All I asked for was a cot in a corner somewhere. (MAURICE *and* DIDIER, *at the foot of the bed, react in horror,* DIDIER *with a wide "take" from* ALICE *almost to the archway.*)

MAURICE. I know. But I said there's nothing too good for my Aunt Alice.

ALICE. So this is where my money goes! Who do you think I am? Madame Pompadour? I like a bed built for character . . . not for the Sport of Kings! (*She pokes the bed with her umbrella.*)

MAURICE. But I did it all for you!

ALICE. All these expensive trappings for a fort-night?

MAURICE. You're going to stay here two weeks?

ALICE. I only hope I've found Rosine by then.

MAURICE. You still don't know where she is?

ALICE. No. When I enquire, all they do is laugh in my face and give me a knowing look . . . as if all the girls who get lost in Paris are bound to be found in the same place . . . a place I know nothing about . . . (*To the audience, sadly perplexed and with tears in her voice.*) and nobody wants to take me to! (*She sits on the pouffe.*)

DIDIER. All the more reason for mademoiselle to continue her search.

MAURICE. A good idea. (*They swoop* ALICE *up and rush her towards the double doors.*) You'll never for-give yourself if you let Rosine spend the night God knows where . . .

DIDIER. With God knows whom!

ALICE. I'm sorry, but it's too late. I've been up since the crack of dawn and I'm exhausted. (*To* DIDIER.) Turn down my bed! (DIDIER *and* MAURICE *look at each other with dismay.*)

DIDIER. Very well, mademoiselle. (*He tosses the*

decorative pillow behind the bed and flips down the cover.)

ALICE. And, of course, I must go to the kitchen to do my toilet for the night?

MAURICE. I'm afraid there's no other place you can go.

ALICE. How chic! To put your toothbrush on the stove.

MAURICE. At least it will be quite safe there.

ALICE. If it doesn't boil over. (*To the audience.*) I'd like to know what they do with the bathroom in this house. (*She goes up the left stairs.*) Sit around the tub and serve dinner, I suppose. (*On the platform, she faces front and shouts:*) There's nobody here! You can come in now! (*She continues on down the right stairs.* DIDIER *looks at her as if she is insane.*) That's because I'm going to the kitchen. It's the rule of the house. (*She goes out through the double doors.*)

MAURICE. Oh God! She's settling in!

DIDIER. (*Desperately.*) Is there any way of keeping her in the kitchen?

MAURICE. Lock her in the refrigerator?

DIDIER. Idiot! (*He quickly takes off the white coat in order to remove the apron.*) I'll keep the white coat. You put the apron back on. (*He gives* MAURICE *the apron.*)

MAURICE. (*Taking off the dinner jacket, in order to put on the apron.*) That's right. We must keep up appearances.

DIDIER. Huguette will be coming in! What a mix-up! (*He puts the white coat back on as he goes out down the hall.*)

MAURICE. (*To the audience, while putting on the apron.*) Everybody will be coming in . . . climbing all

over each other! (*There is a knock on the bedroom
door.*) There's one already! Just a second . . . one
second! (Rosine *comes in from the bedroom wearing
a seductive negligee.*) Oh! Mademoiselle . . .

Rosine. (*Coming down the stairs.*) What are you
doing here? Where are they?

Maurice. Who?

Rosine. Why, Maurice de Corneblanche . . . and
Clara.

Maurice. . . . They'll be back.

Rosine. (*Beckoning him over with her finger.*) Come
over here. I can see you're really a very sympathetic
young man and I would like you to do me a very
special favor. (*Smitten,* Maurice *goes to* Rosine.)

Maurice. Oh, anything, mademoiselle!

Rosine. Prevent Monsieur de Corneblanche from
spending the night with that Clara person!

Maurice. But why should that upset mademoiselle?
Just between us, he's not very interesting.

Rosine. I have my reasons. (Didier *comes in from
the hall wearing the white coat.*)

Didier. (*Seeing* Rosine.) Oh! (*Then noticing her
negligee.*) Uh-oh!

Rosine. (*Noticing his white servant's coat.*) Why
the masquerade?

Didier. (*Who had forgotten he's wearing it.*) Masquerade?

Rosine. The coat . . . the white coat.

Didier. (*Disturbed.*) Oh! Yes! Of course . . . the
coat. Whatever made me put it on?

Maurice. I can't imagine.

Didier. (*To* Maurice.) You fool! You hung it
where I hang my pajama coat and I made a mistake
in the dark. (Didier *takes off the white coat and*

passes it to MAURICE, *who tosses it on the bed.* DIDIER *puts on the dinner jacket, which* MAURICE *had taken off.* ROSINE *makes herself alluringly comfortable on the chaise.*)

MAURICE. There we are then!

ROSINE. (*To* MAURICE, *pointedly.*) Well, good night.

MAURICE. I . . . I . . . (*He doesn't want to leave them together.*) Good night, mademoiselle. (*He reluctantly leaves down the hall.* DIDIER *looks tenderly at* ROSINE *and sits close beside her.* MAURICE *re-enters. He comes down quietly and sits on the foot of the chaise; then facing the audience, says disarmingly:*) I don't feel sleepy.

DIDIER. (*Rising. Irritably.*) You must be. You've been on the go all day!

MAURICE. (*Good humored. Smiling.*) Monsieur doesn't have to be afraid of keeping me up. I can stay here all night, if necessary.

DIDIER. You're wanted in the kitchen. (*He pushes* MAURICE *up towards the double doors.*) You understand what I mean by in the kitchen!

MAURICE. Oh, the kitchen. In the kitchen. (*He stops to look at* ROSINE.) Oh, God! Well! (*He leaves.*)

DIDIER. (*Switching off the main light. To* ROSINE.) Why the masquerade?

ROSINE. Masquerade?

DIDIER. The negligee. It's amazing the way it reveals and conceals at the same time.

ROSINE. Even on a silly white goose from the provinces?

DIDIER. (*Sitting on the chaise.*) Silly white goose? Tonight, Rosine, you're a desirable *woman.* Here, in this room, with the flames casting shadows on your warm, satin skin, I know now you're the woman I came here to love.

ROSINE. Oh, Maurice, you *are* a monster!

DIDIER. A sinner, perhaps. A sinner with a soul that only you can redeem. But not a monster.

ROSINE. Oh, Maurice, can I really believe what you tell me?

DIDIER. Every last word.

ROSINE. You wouldn't lie to me? I am a desirable woman?

DIDIER. The most desirable woman I have ever met. (*She rises and goes almost to the center of the room.*)

ROSINE. Oh, if I'm not careful, I'll be believing this is true!

DIDIER. It is.

ROSINE. Darling, I can see it so clearly . . . a lovely vision! We were married this morning and this is our wedding night. I'm about to take off my bridal gown and you are about to discover those treasures which now belong to you!

DIDIER. Rosine, dearest. (ROSINE *slips out of her negligee.* DIDIER *is left holding it, dumbfounded at this turn in events.*)

ROSINE. (*Lying on the chaise.*) Yes, it is our wedding night and I'm waiting for you to take me in your arms! (DIDIER *quickly tosses the negligee on the stand which formerly held the rubber plant. He can't get to* ROSINE *fast enough.*)

DIDIER. I love you, Rosine, love you!

ROSINE. Oh, darling, how I've longed for this moment!

DIDIER. My dearest darling . . . Give me your lips!

ROSINE. (*Protesting, her face to the audience.*) No, I mustn't! (*Then yielding.*) Take them!

DIDIER. Rosine, darling! (*He kisses her lips.*) Such beautiful lips . . . so fresh . . . so soft . . . so yielding . . . (*Holding both her hands, he is slowly drawing her to the bed.*) Come . . . come . . .

ROSINE. Yes! Yes! (*She takes away her hands. He goes sprawling on the bed. She laughs in his face, then switches on the main light.*) You're very funny! Good night! Sleep well. Your dream bride is off to dream alone! (*She goes up the right stairs, taking the negligee with her.*)

DIDIER. Rosine . . . you're not leaving me?

ROSINE. Oh, yes, monsieur. I only wanted to show you what you might have had.

DIDIER. (*Agonized.*) Oh, no!

ROŞINE. Oh, yes. All that and a little bit more! (*She goes into the bedroom laughing at his dismay.*)

DIDIER. (*Rushing up the right stairs, trying to stop her.*) Rosine! Rosine! (*The bedroom door slams in his face.*) So you think you can make a fool of me? Well, you'll be sorry! (*He comes down the left stairs, taking off his dinner jacket, which he puts on the pouffe.*) There are other women in this house just as desirable. And I'm going to take the first one who comes in! (*The double doors open.* ALICE *comes in, wearing a long flannel nightgown, with her hair in curlers and carrying her umbrella.*) No! Not the first . . . the *second!* (MAURICE *has followed* ALICE *into the room.* DIDIER, *in dismay, is leaning on the centerpiece of the pouffe, his back to* ALICE. *She pokes him with the umbrella.*)

ALICE. (*Seeing* DIDIER *in his shirtsleeves.*) So now you're undressing in my room!

DIDIER. Me?

ALICE. Where's your coat?

MAURICE. Your white coat, my man. Your white coat. Where have you put it?

DIDIER. How do I know?

ALICE. Well, you should know! It's your place to know!

MAURICE. (*Going to the bed for the white coat.*) Here it is. Put it on! (DIDIER *puts on the coat.*)

ALICE. You couldn't get a job in the provinces!

MAURICE. (*In his shirtsleeves, he picks up the dinner jacket from the pouffe and puts it on.*) I wouldn't engage him for the pigs!

ALICE. Now if you'll both be good enough to leave, I'll go to bed.

DIDIER. Mademoiselle is going to bed?

ALICE. Unless you prefer I stand on the dressing table and sing the Jewel Song from 'Faust'.

DIDIER. No, no, no, no, no!

MAURICE. How about going to a midnight movie?

ALICE. With my hair in curlers?

MAURICE. They're very becoming.

ALICE. Stop these stupidities and take yourselves elsewhere so I can get some sleep! (*She sits on the chaise, placing the umbrella beside her.*)

DIDIER. Mademoiselle will have no trouble sleeping here.

MAURICE. Everybody is very quiet.

DIDIER. Nobody will disturb mademoiselle.

MAURICE. Nobody.

ALICE. (*Who has taken off her slippers, crosses her legs and manipulates one foot with her hands, turning it in a circle, to ease the pain.*) I should hope not. That would be the last straw.

MAURICE. Then we'll leave you. (*He doesn't budge.*)

ALICE. (*The same business with the other foot.*)

That's that, then. (*Sarcastically.*) Unless you'd like to tuck me in? (*Side by side,* MAURICE *and* DIDIER *reluctantly back up towards the archway.*)

MAURICE. Then . . . we'll . . . leave her.

DIDIER. Yes, I'm afraid we'll have to.

MAURICE. Good night.

DIDIER. (*Sympathetically.*) And so Maurice, we say good night and farewell to your lovely inheritance. (*He switches off the main light. They leave down the hall.*)

ALICE. (*Alone.*) Oh! Men! What a pack of good-for-nothings! I'm thankful I never permitted one to get into my bed! (*She rises.*) Poor Rosine. I wonder where she's sleeping? Well, we'll worry about that tomorrow. It's too late now. Into bed you go, Alice. (*She climbs into bed and switches off the headboard light. The boudoir door opens quietly.* GASTON's *head appears. He looks cautiously in the direction of the bedroom, then turns and comes down the stairs. He is wearing pajamas. He takes a perfume bottle with an atomizer from his pocket and sprays himself and the area around him. Then, he takes off his slippers and gets into bed with* ALICE.)

GASTON. Coucou!

ALICE. What? What is it?

GASTON. It is I, angel. Your fifteen minutes are up.

ALICE. (*From the far right side of the bed, she peers out from behind the covers.*) Oh, my God! It's a man!

GASTON. Your man, good girl! It's time.

ALICE. Time? Time for what? (*She switches on the headboard light.*) You!

GASTON. You!

ALICE. So that's it! I am Madame Pompadour!

GASTON. Yes! Yes! You're Madame Pompadour. I'm glad you've been revived!

ALICE. What are you doing here, getting into bed when someone else is there?

GASTON. But after all, madame, this is my house.

ALICE. I see! It's a trap! What are you going to do to me?

GASTON. Nothing. Nothing at all, I assure you.

ALICE. Don't touch me or I'll scream the house down!

GASTON. Believe me, you're in no danger.

ALICE. That's what you say.

GASTON. I was merely passing by and said to myself: 'Gaston, why don't you get into bed?'

ALICE. With me?

GASTON. No! You're the last person I was thinking of!

ALICE. That's better, considering we only met this afternoon. (GASTON *moves.*) Don't move! Stay still!

GASTON. (*Pointing right.*) If madame will permit, I should like to get out of bed.

ALICE. (*'Crossing swords' with* GASTON *by pointing left.*) That way! Not over me! (*At this moment,* DIDIER *comes in from the hall.*)

DIDIER. (*Seeing them in bed.*) Oh!!!

ALICE. Oh!

GASTON. Oh! (ALICE *and* GASTON *lie back, pulling the blanket over their faces.*)

DIDIER. Oh! (*He goes out down the hall, startled at what he's seen.*)

ALICE. (*Sitting up.*) Oh! I'm dishonored! He saw me with you!

GASTON. I'm afraid he did. (*He gets out of bed and*

puts on his slippers.) But don't worry, I'll explain everything to him. He'll forgive you.

ALICE. He'll forgive me! Who'll forgive me?

GASTON. He will. The one who just surprised us.

ALICE. That butler! You'll ask him to forgive me?

GASTON. What butler?

ALICE. The one who just came in.

GASTON. (*To the audience.*) The strain's becoming too much for her. (*To* ALICE, *tragically.*) That man is your lover.

ALICE. (*Indignantly.*) What did you say? How dare you! (*She gets up on her knees and holds the blanket up to her chin.*) I'm a virgin and proud of it! A gold medal virgin, do you hear? And don't ask to see my ribbons!

GASTON. That won't be necessary.

ALICE. I've never been anyone's mistress, least of all a butler's!

GASTON. (*Wagging his head despairingly.*) She's lost her mind.

ALICE. My mind is intact! (*Slapping the bed furiously.*) Apologise, do you hear? Apologise!

GASTON. Of course. Calm down.

ALICE. I'll calm down when you clear out!

GASTON. (*Going backwards up the stairs.*) I'm going. I'm going.

ALICE. Not fast enough!

GASTON. (*Suddenly angry, he comes back down the stairs.*) Be quiet! Listen to me!

ALICE. (*Aghast.*) What? (*He goes past the right side of the bed and points towards the study.*)

GASTON. (*With authority.*) That's where you're supposed to be sleeping! The man you're waiting for is in there!

ALICE. What's that?

GASTON. You heard me.

ALICE. (*Seizing her umbrella.*) I've heard enough! One more word and I'll crack Napoleon over your head! Get out! (*She gets out of the bed and chases* GASTON, *who runs wildly up the right stairs.*)

GASTON. Whatever you say! Whatever you say! (*He goes into the boudoir threatened by the umbrella.*)

ALICE. (*Alone.*) Repulsive man! I should have gone to bed with my clothes on. (*She comes back to the bed.*) I'd have been safer in the kitchen . . . (*She gets into bed and sniffs* GASTON's *pillow.*) And he was perfumed, no less! . . . scented from top to bottom . . . everything to seduce me! The street Arab! (*She switches off the headboard light. In the semidarkness,* HUGUETTE *opens the bedroom door. At the same moment,* CLARA *comes in from the study. They take off their negligees and slip into bed on either side of* ALICE. *They lie down. Silence.*)

HUGUETTE. It's me! I'm here! I've come!

CLARA. No-o . . . it's me. *I'm* here. *I've* come.

ALICE. (*With the blanket covering her face, she comes up very slowly. Then, her eyes are seen, peering over the blanket.*) What? What is it now?

HUGUETTE. Who is it?

ALICE. Rape! Rape! (*She switches on the headboard light.* ALICE, HUGUETTE *and* CLARA *sit up and scream.*)

HUGUETTE. A woman!

CLARA. Two women!

ALICE. Three women! By Saint Peter and Saint Paul, everybody is having a rendezvous under my eiderdown!

HUGUETTE. What are you two doing here?

CLARA. It seems to me I should be asking you that question!

ALICE. And me? I should take this as being perfectly natural, I suppose!

HUGUETTE. This is not a hotel!

ALICE. (*To* HUGUETTE.) Let us proceed in order. First, who are you?

HUGUETTE. I am Madame Dubois, the mistress of this house.

ALICE. Delighted to meet you. (*She shakes hands with* HUGUETTE. *Then, to* CLARA.) And you?

CLARA. Me? I'm neither a mistress nor a madame.

ALICE. Don't give up hope. Anything's possible in this house.

HUGUETTE. (*To* ALICE.) What I'd like to know is how you got in here?

ALICE. Not down the chimney, you can be sure of that. (MAURICE *comes in from the hall.*)

MAURICE. (*Seeing them in bed, he pulls up short.*) Oh, my God! (*And runs towards the study.*)

ALICE, HUGUETTE, CLARA. Oh!!! (*They lie back and pull the blanket over their heads.* MAURICE *goes into the study.* ALICE, HUGUETTE *and* CLARA *sit up again.*)

HUGUETTE. (*To* ALICE.) I ask you again, who invited you here?

ALICE. (*Pointing to the study.*) If you must know, he did!

HUGUETTE. Who? That person who just came in?

ALICE. Yes. That person, as you call him.

HUGUETTE. (*Getting out of the bed and putting on her negligee.*) He dares to invite people to my house! . . . Then you're the butler's mistress!

ALICE. (*Outraged.*) *What?!* (CLARA *bounces out of the bed and puts on her negligee.*)

HUGUETTE. (*To* ALICE.) Will you have the decency to get out of that bed and into the kitchen!

ALICE. (*Getting out of the bed and staggering downstage.*) The kitchen! The kitchen! Always the kitchen! (*She fetches her slippers and umbrella.*)

CLARA. (*To* HUGUETTE.) She's obviously a bit mental. (*To* ALICE.) There, there!

ALICE. (*Alarmed, she uses her umbrella like a sword on* CLARA.) Stay away from me! (CLARA, *frightened, jumps back.*)

HUGUETTE. (*On the other side of* ALICE.) There, there!

ALICE. (*Doing the same umbrella business to* HUGUETTE.) You, too! (*She backs up the right stairs.*) I see what the trouble is. You're all suffering from the same thing in this house! You think every woman has a butler for a lover! (CLARA *and* HUGUETTE *are convinced* ALICE *is crazy and vice versa.*)

HUGUETTE. In your case, I can well believe it.

ALICE. All right. Let's say it's true.

CLARA. You admit it?

ALICE. (*On the platform, leaning over the railing.*) It's impossible to deny it!

HUGUETTE. (*Crying out.*) You've had a rendezvous with him?

ALICE. If you say so.

CLARA. Then you are his mistress?

ALICE. Yes, yes! I admit it! I'm the butler's mistress! (*Coming down the left stairs.*) I'm the mistress of every butler in France and Navarre! I'm the Queen of Spain, pining for the love of her lackey. Ruy Blas is waiting for me . . . down by the coffee mill . . . (*Pointing with her umbrella to the double doors.*) in the kitchen, of course! . . . Yes, I'm the Queen of

Spain! Ole! Ole! (*She goes out through the double doors.*)

CLARA. Do you think she's dangerous?

HUGUETTE. I'm going to call the police. (*She goes to the telephone on the dressing table.*)

CLARA. Yes! Oh, no! Don't! Let the butler take care of her. The police, tonight, will only complicate things.

HUGUETTE. Perhaps you're right.

CLARA. As for me, this madwoman's arrival has been a godsend. I was about to do something very foolish. But I'm cured of him now.

HUGUETTE. Really?

CLARA. If you want to sleep in this bed, you're welcome to it. I'm going to sleep in the study. Good night, madame. (*She goes into the study.*)

HUGUETTE. Good night! (*To the audience.*) What shall I do? He may still come looking for her. Well, if Providence sees fit I sacrifice myself for Rosine, then I'm ready! (*She takes off her negligee, gets into bed and lies down. Then she pops back up.*) It's a wonderful feeling knowing you're going to do something for somebody else! (*She switches off the headboard light. She hears a door opening.*) Here he is! (GASTON *comes in from the boudoir. He looks cautiously over to the bedroom door, then comes quietly down the right stairs. He sprays himself again with the perfume before removing his slippers and getting into bed.*)

GASTON. (*Touching* HUGUETTE's *head.*) Oh, I can feel somebody's pretty curls . . . and this time there are no curling pins. Darling! (*With his hand outside the blanket, he touches a different part of her body with each amorous:*) Oh! . . . Oh! . . . Oh! (*Until he reaches her bottom and recognizes it.*) Uh-oh! (*He picks up the blanket and hides his guilty face.*)

HUGUETTE. Gaston! (*She switches on the headboard light. They sit up and stare at each other with dismay.*)

GASTON. (*Fanning himself with his end of the blanket.*) You . . . of all people!

HUGUETTE. And you.

GASTON. Who did you think it was?

HUGUETTE. Who did *you* think it was?

GASTON. Me? I thought it was you.

HUGUETTE. I was certain it was you. (GASTON *laughs nervously.*)

GASTON. (*Not very certain of himself.*) Darling!

HUGUETTE. (*Not very certain of herself.*) Darling!

GASTON. This is where we came in.

HUGUETTE. Yes. Isn't it strange we both should have had the same idea?

GASTON. (*Getting out of bed.*) At the same time too! I am surprised!

HUGUETTE. (*Getting out of bed.*) So am I. Very surprised indeed!

GASTON. If you were looking for me, why did you come in here and not the boudoir? Huguette, I think you're lying! (*He sits at the foot of the bed.*)

HUGUETTE. (*Brusquely.*) What do you think I think you're doing? (*She sits beside him and melts.*) Oh, Gaston, let's be honest with each other. We've had a narrow escape.

GASTON. You know, Huguette, I love only you. It's these interpolers who are to blame. We were perfectly content until they moved in.

HUGUETTE. Content? We were unconscious! They reminded us of what we've been neglecting. (*They are holding hands.*) Gaston, I wonder what would happen if we got back into bed and put out the light.

GASTON. I wonder. Shall we see? (*They get back into bed.* GASTON *switches off the headboard light and takes* HUGUETTE *into his arms.* CLARA *comes in quietly from the study,* MAURICE *following her. She starts to get into the bed. The occupants scream. At the same moment,* MAURICE *switches on the main light.*)

CLARA. Oh, I beg your pardon. I thought this bed might still be free. (HUGUETTE *and* GASTON *scramble out of the bed.*)

GASTON. You can have it. We don't mind sleeping elsewhere. (*Looking at* HUGUETTE.) As long as we're together.

CLARA. Something wonderful's happened!

MAURICE. We're going round and round the southern belt on the honeymoon express! (*Enchanted.*) Toot! Toot! (*He choo-choo train shuffles* CLARA *around a chair.*)

CLARA. (*Lovingly.*) Toot! Toot!

HUGUETTE. (*Astonished.*) Toot, toot?

GASTON. (*Furiously.*) What's all this toot, toot? (ALICE *comes in through the double doors, followed by* DIDIER *wearing the white coat.*)

ALICE. Toot, toot! Toot, toot! Listen to them! I told you they're all mad!

HUGUETTE. The butler's mistress! She's back!

ALICE. Here we go again! Hasn't my nephew told you yet who I am? I am the aunt of Maurice de Corneblanche!

GASTON. (*To* DIDIER.) What? You're her nephew? Her lover? And a butler?

DIDIER. Yes, that is . . . I mean . . . (*Looking at* ALICE.) No!

ALICE. (*Indicating* MAURICE.) Maurice, my nephew, is this one!

GASTON. What?

HUGUETTE. The butler's your nephew?

ALICE. (*Infuriated.*) Everybody's got butlers on the brain!

CLARA. (*Pointing to* MAURICE.) But he's Didier, the novelist.

ALICE. (*Pointing to* MAURICE.) No. He's Maurice!

CLARA. (*To* ALICE, *indicating* DIDIER.) Then this one is Didier?

ALICE. How should I know?

DIDIER. Yes, I'm Didier.

MAURICE. Yes, he's Didier.

GASTON. Then what are you doing in my home impersonating each other?

MAURICE. (*Like a bad boy caught in some mischief.*) It was his idea. He's to blame.

DIDIER. Yes, I created the situation in order to write a love story. I imagined myself in love with madame . . . (*He nods towards* HUGUETTE.)

HUGUETTE. (*With false indignation.*) Oh! What a colossal nerve!

DIDIER. (*To* HUGUETTE.) I made a bet I could spend one night with you . . . madame!

GASTON. (*Furiously.*) I demand an explanation! From both of you!

MAURICE. (*Indicating* CLARA.) I wouldn't be too demanding in that direction, old boy!

GASTON. (*With his hands to his ears, making them flap, as he moves away.*) Oh!!!

HUGUETTE. (*Reprimanding.*) Gaston! (*But they will soon smile at each other again.*)

ALICE. Maurice, you've become involved in a singularly immoral adventure!

MAURICE. How can it be immoral, auntie, when nobody is sleeping with anybody he shouldn't be?

CLARA. I found a man I really like. And he's unattached!

MAURICE. It struck us while we were choo-choochooing through a tunnel. You wanted me to marry, auntie. Well, rejoice! I'm marrying Clara!

ALICE. (*Moving away from* MAURICE.) How can I rejoice without Rosine . . . the girl you drove to her doom! (ROSINE *comes in from the bedroom.*)

DIDIER. (*To* ALICE.) Don't worry, mademoiselle. Rosine will be well looked after.

ROSINE. (*Seeing* ALICE.) Why, mademoiselle! (*She comes down the left stairs.*)

ALICE. What? (*Seeing* ROSINE.) You! Oh, I'm going to faint! (*Everyone flees and hides as though a bomb is about to fall. With no one to catch her,* ALICE *doesn't faint. Everyone comes out of his hiding place.*) Rosine! You! Here! A sister virgin loose in this butler's playground! Why did you run away to Paris?

ROSINE. To find a fiance.

DIDIER. And she did! (*He opens his arms to* ROSINE.)

ROSINE. Oh! Maurice!

GASTON. No! No! No! Not Maurice. He's Didier. (*Indicating the correct personnages.*) Maurice . . . the vicomte. Didier . . . the story teller.

ROSINE. (*To* GASTON.) I don't care. He can change his name as often as he likes . . . after he's changed mine.

DIDIER. (*To* ROSINE.) Didier Larue is yours forever, my sweet.

GASTON. Good. Can we all go to bed now?

HUGUETTE. I'd like nothing better. (HUGUETTE *and* GASTON *go up the right stairs to the platform.*)

CLARA. I was thinking the same thing. (*She takes* MAURICE *by the hand and rushes him towards the study.*) Get out your whistle, Maurice! Toot! Toot!

MAURICE. (*To the audience.*) This is going to be the first time a woman has found wedded bliss with a human chastity belt! (CLARA *and* MAURICE *go happily into the study.*)

ALICE. (*Going up the left stairs.*) Rosine, are you sleeping in here? (*She indicates the bedroom.*)

ROSINE. Yes, mademoiselle.

ALICE. Then it's time we went to bed. Come along, little vagabond. (ROSINE *goes up the left stairs.* DIDIER *starts to follow her.* ALICE *points her umbrella at him.*) Stay where you are or you'll have me and Napoleon to contend with! (ROSINE *goes into the bedroom. To* GASTON *and* HUGUETTE.) Tell me, does this apartment really belong to you?

GASTON. That *was* our impression.

ALICE. Then thanks for the use of the community kitchen. Oh, one thing more. There's nothing I need, so stay out of my bed . . . all of you! (*She goes into the bedroom.*)

DIDIER. Monsieur, have you any further need of me?

GASTON. Hardly! (*He kisses* HUGUETTE.)

HUGUETTE. Pleasant dreams! (*She goes into the boudoir.*)

GASTON. Yes, pleasant dreams. (*He comes down the right stairs.*) You'll find the Ovaltine in the study!

DIDIER. Thank you. To think I had three women . . . ready, willing and eager . . . and I end up spending the night alone. (ROSINE *comes in from the bedroom.*)

GASTON. Rosine! What are you doing here?

ROSINE. I crept back, monsieur, to tell Didier I love him.

GASTON. Well, say it quickly before Napoleon starts up the Battle of Waterloo again! (ROSINE *comes down the left stairs and goes to* DIDIER.)

DIDIER. Rosine . . . one kiss . . . just one kiss! (*To* GASTON.) All right with you?

GASTON. All right. Just one. (DIDIER *kisses* ROSINE.)

VOICE OF ALICE. (*Off-stage, from the bedroom.*) Rosine!

GASTON. (*Shouting, as he grabs hold of the bedroom doorknob.*) No! No! No! You can't come in!

VOICE OF ALICE. (*Off-stage, from the bedroom.*) Why can't I come in?

GASTON. (*Motioning to the lovers to hide.*) Because . . . *because* . . . BECAUSE . . . (ROSINE *and* DIDIER *have scrambled into the bed, pulling the blanket over them.*) There's nobody here! You can come in now! (ALICE *comes in from the bedroom. She comes down the stairs, across the room, and out through the double doors to the kitchen. Meanwhile,* GASTON *has come to the center of the room. To the audience.*) It's the rule of the house!

CURTAIN

PROPERTY PLOT

2 vases of red roses
vase with a single red rose
very tall rubber plant
a tray with coffee service for two:
  coffee pot, cups and saucers, teaspoons, sugar
  bowl, sugar tongs
a pair of white servant's gloves (Maurice)
telephone
hand bell for summoning butler
gold cigarette case
a fifty franc note
handkerchief (Maurice)
envelope with will inside
business card
overnight bag
3 suitcases
feather duster
telegram in envelope
a wrapped package of Ovaltine
franc notes of various denominations
Gladstone bag
umbrella with a Napoleon head
a pair of ladies' brown suede gloves (Aunt Alice)
log carrier with logs
water carafe and glass
perfume bottle with atomizer

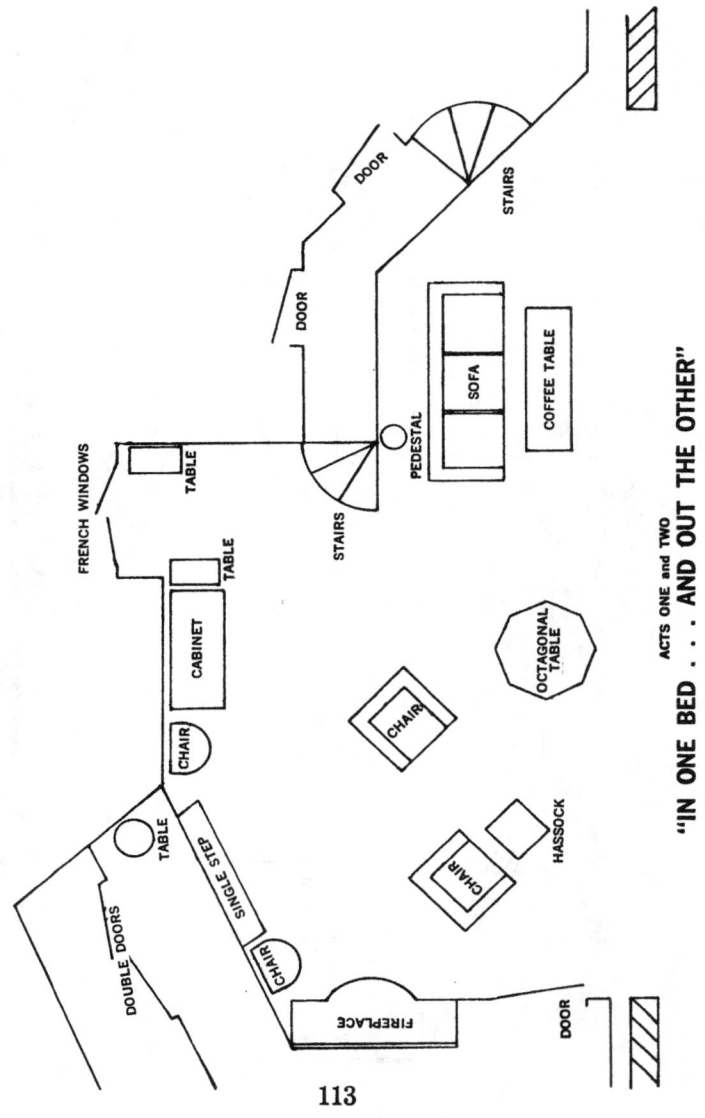

ACTS ONE and TWO
"IN ONE BED . . . AND OUT THE OTHER"

113

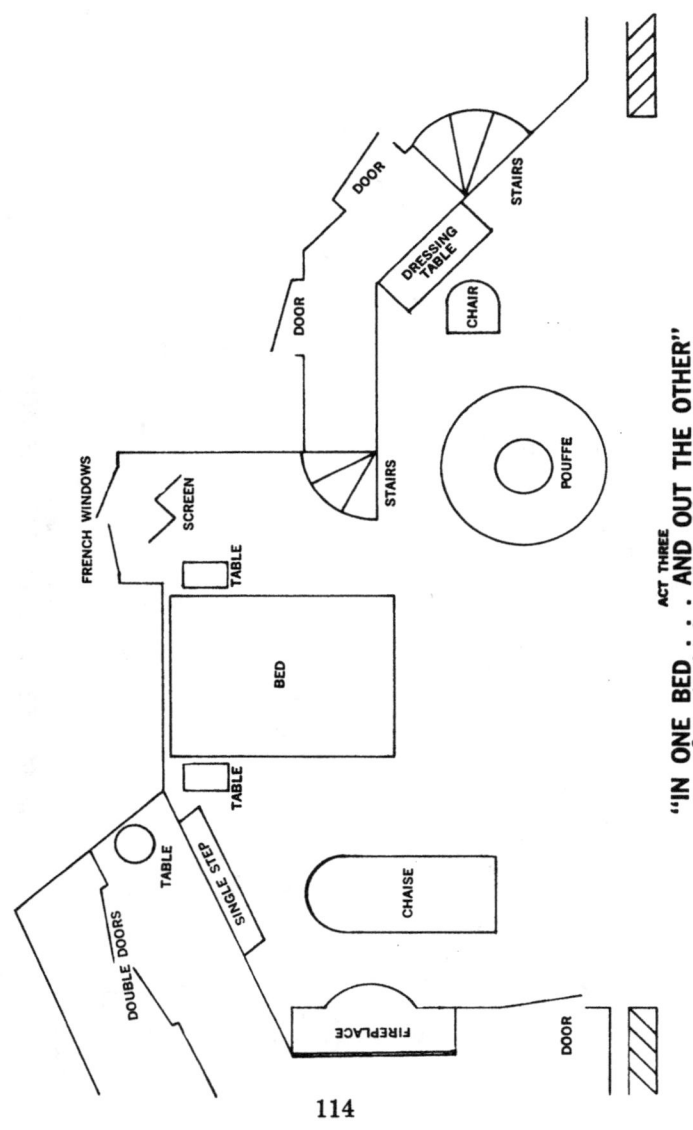

ACT THREE
"IN ONE BED . . . AND OUT THE OTHER"
Same set as Acts One and Two with Furniture Changed

114

Also By

Mawby Green and Ed Feilbert

13 RUE DE L'AMOUR

DING DONG DEAD

PAJAMA TOPS

ABOUT THE ADAPTERS

The first collaboration of **Mawby Green** and **Ed Feilbert** was a dramatization of the Elizabeth Bowen novel THE HOUSE IN PARIS. The production introduced Ludmilla Pitoeff to American audiences, the late Mme. Pitoeff being George Bernard Shaw's French SAINT JOAN. Her leading man in HOUSE was a young actor, Yul Brynner.

Adaptations of two hit French farces by Jean de Letraz followed. IN ONE BED...AND OUT THE OTHER, heralded as a "laughter explosion," successfully toured the U.S., Canada, England and South Africa and is a tremendous audience-pleaser whenever and wherever it plays. PAJAMA TOPS is one of the longest running comedies ever produced, with five coast-to-coast U.S. tours, a six-year run in London, four tours in England, three in South Africa, two in Australia and is a perennial summer attraction in the British seaside resorts. The cable TV version, produced by Lorimar/Showtime, stars Robert Klein, Susan George and Pia Zadora.

Their 13 RUE DE L'AMOUR, based on a Feydeau farce, brought Leslie Caron and Louis Jourdan back together again for the first time since the film GIGI. Together the stars enjoyed a huge success in the Chicago production and 10-week Australian tour, but have not been free of commitments at the same time long enough for an open-end run, consequently, M. Jourdan appeared without Mme. Caron in both the London and Broadway productions. This adaptation of the uproarious Feydeau romp continues to delight in stock, amateur and regional theatres.

Leslie Caron has since enchanted summer theatre audiences in another Green/Feilbert adaptation, ONE FOR THE TANGO.

THE DECORATOR
Donald Churchill

Comedy / 1m, 2f / Interior

Marcia returns to her flat to find it has not been painted as she arranged. A part time painter who is filling in for an ill colleague is just beginning the work when the wife of the man with whom Marcia is having an affair arrives to tell all to Marcia's husband. Marcia hires the painter a part time actor to impersonate her husband at the confrontation. Hilarity is piled upon hilarity as the painter, who takes his acting very seriously, portrays the absent husband. The wronged wife decides that the best revenge is to sleep with Marcia's husband, an ecstatic experience for them both. When Marcia learns that the painter/actor has slept with her rival, she demands the opportunity to show him what really good sex is.

"Irresistible."
– London Daily Telegraph

"This play will leave you rolling in the aisles....
I all but fell from my seat laughing."
– London Star

PERFECT WEDDING
Robin Hawdon

Comedy / 2m, 4f / Interior

A man wakes up in the bridal suite on his wedding morning to find an extremely attractive naked girl in bed beside him. In the depths of a stag night hangover, he can't even remember meeting her. Before he can get her out, his bride to be arrives to dress for the wedding. In the ensuing panic, the girl is locked in the bathroom. The best man is persuaded to claim her, but he gets confused and introduces the chamber maid to the bride as his date. The crisis escalates to nuclear levels by the time the mother of the bride and the best man's actual girlfriend arrive. This rare combination of riotous farce and touching love story has provoked waves of laughter across Europe and America.

"Laughs abound."
– *Wisconsin Advocate*

"The full house audience roared with delight."
– *Green Bay Gazette*